SPELLS AND SUBTERFUGE

BETH DOLGNER

Spells and Subterfuge
Crones of a Feather Paranormal Cozy Mysteries, Book One

© 2025 Beth Dolgner

Ebook ISBN-13: 978-1-958587-36-2
Print ISBN-13: 978-1-958587-37-9

Spells and Subterfuge is a work of fiction. Names, characters, places, and incidents either are the products of the author's imagination or are used fictitiously. Any resemblance to actual persons, living or dead, businesses, companies, events, or locales is entirely coincidental.

Published by Redglare Press

Cover Design: Melody Simmons

https://bethdolgner.com

contents

one

I WAS LYING ON my back on the floor, my head and shoulders completely inside the cabinet under the kitchen sink, when I heard footsteps creaking across the pine boards.

I had thought I was home alone.

There was absolutely no way I could extract myself from my spot fast enough to confront whomever was coming toward me, but I forced down my worry. *It's probably the electrician*, I told myself. *Maybe I forgot he was coming this morning.*

"Hey, Archer," I called, my voice echoing in the tiny cabinet space. "Do you know anything about fixing leaks?" I impatiently tapped a fingernail against the metal pipe. "Maybe I'm not as handy as I thought."

I'd learned to be pretty self-sufficient during the past ten years of living alone, but some things were still outside my skill range.

Apparently, fixing a leaky sink was one of those things.

Instead of Archer's deep timbre, I heard a woman's melodic voice. "You must be Hazel! Do you still have a room available?"

I craned my head toward the voice, but all I saw was a piece of paper waving wildly in my direction. "I am, and I do. Hang on. This won't be pretty."

With a few grunts, and one groan when one of my ample hips smacked against the cabinet door, I wiggled my top half out of the cabinet and moved into a sitting position on the floor.

My visitor seemed to take that as an invitation, because she gracefully lowered herself until she was sitting across from me. Her long black braids swung with the motion, and I smiled to see bright-purple streaks coursing through some of them.

"I knew it!" The woman smiled triumphantly, her dark-brown eyes lighting up. "I was certain I'd get one of the available rooms. Oh, I'm Josephine Davenport, but you can call me Jo. Just don't call me Josie, okay? There's only one person who ever got to call me that, and he—well, that's another story. Tell me about the room."

I couldn't help the small laugh that escaped my lips. Jo was a bundle of energy, but I liked her instantly. There was something slightly chaotic about her, but at the same time, she was looking at me with kindness and excitement.

And no judgment. Maybe that's why I like her.

"I still have all three rooms available," I told Jo. "But, I just submitted the classified ad to the newspaper yesterday afternoon, so how do you already know I'm looking for renters?"

Jo grinned. "I write for the paper, and I saw your ad this morning on my editor's desk. And I know you're going to accept me as a renter, because I wrote about it!" Jo waved the sheet of paper toward me again, and I caught sight of hand-written lines of text.

My eyebrows drew down. "You wrote a newspaper article about moving in here?"

"No, I wrote an intention." Jo's hand stilled so I could see the words written on the paper. The first sentence read, *Hazel Underwood is going to tell me she's happy to have me as a renter.*

"You used magic to make sure you'd get one of my available rooms." I nodded, as if that was normal to me. At the same time, I reminded myself it was going to take a while to get used to living in Foxfire Haven again, where something as simple as deciding on a paint color for a bedroom might involve a spell of decision.

"I'm great at manifesting magic," Jo clarified. "What I write becomes reality. I've been wanting a new place to live, and this seems like a perfect setup, so I wrote about how much you'd like me, and how much I'll enjoy living here. Though, I have to admit, I never thought I'd be excited about living in a funeral home."

"Former funeral home. And I never thought I'd live here, either. Still, it was my uncle's home for decades. If it worked for him, I'm sure it will work for me, too."

My rear end was beginning to protest about the hard floor, so I stood slowly. "I can give you a tour, if you like, but be forewarned, it's a work in progress. I've only been here a few weeks, so I still have a lot of work to do."

Jo rose easily, then brushed off the back of her houndstooth pants. For good measure, she ran a hand down the front of her mustard-yellow silk blouse, too. I couldn't blame her: there was still a lot of dust floating around the kitchen.

As I began to lead the way from the kitchen to the available bedrooms, Jo said casually, "Everyone in town has been talking about you since you showed up. The more you keep to yourself, the more we gossip!"

"I'm not being anti-social on purpose." I could hear the defensiveness in my tone. I could also hear the lie.

"It takes time to settle in. I figure you'll get out once you have a handle on this place." We were in a long hallway with faded floral wallpaper, and Jo paused to brush a cobweb off a gilt frame showcasing a painting of a stern-looking man. I had no idea who he was, or why he had deserved a place of honor on the wall.

"Once I came back to this town, I got a little over-whelmed by the amount of work this place needs," I admitted. "I realized I would need roommates if I was going to afford all the renovations. I'll need to find some work, too. A part-time job, at least. Hopefully, I can make this place a nice home for some other old ladies, like me."

Jo snorted. "We are not old! I'm only fifty-four. But I do like your plan. This is going to be a fantastic old-crones home."

I pretended to shudder. My shoulder-length hair was more gray than dark-blond now, and I gave it a quick pat. "I'm not sure I'm ready to be labeled a crone just yet. I'm not even as old as you!" I winked at Jo. "You have a year on me."

"It's not a label. It's a privilege. We're the ones who have wisdom and experience."

"That's a good way of looking at it. Oh, watch your step here." We turned into another, wider hallway that formed a *T* with the one that led from the kitchen. I had propped open the double doors at the junction, giving a long view of the burgundy carpet that ran the length of the hall toward the front door, but the floor dipped slightly where the doors normally stood closed. They had divided the public side of the funeral home—including two chapels—from the side where my uncle had both lived and tended to the dead.

Thinking about the living and the dead was a good reminder about something I had to discuss with Jo, even before we talked about the cost of rent. "You should know this place is haunted," I cautioned.

Jo looked around, as if she expected a ghost to pop up at that moment to make an introduction. "But weren't people already dead when they showed up here? Why would a ghost haunt a funeral home?"

"Holman was the funeral director here in the nineteen twenties and thirties. There were several more directors before my uncle took over, but Holman says he's the only one who stuck around."

Jo waved a hand. "Supernatural stuff doesn't bother me. As long as Holman doesn't wake me up in the middle of the night or interrupt my morning shower, we'll get along just fine."

Of the three rooms I was renting out, two were at the front of the building, one on each side of the hallway. Jo inspected the one on the left, gasping with delight at the three stained-glass windows along one wall. Red, blue, and yellow patches of light danced across the bare floors.

"See the way the ceiling above the windows is arched?" I pointed, then lowered my finger to the spot directly below the arch. "That's where caskets were displayed for funerals. The rest of the room would be filled with chairs."

Jo nodded. "Oh, yeah. I have vague memories of coming to my grandpa's funeral here. The room across the hall is nearly identical, right?"

"Right. It seems ambitious to think a town this small would need to host two funerals simultaneously, doesn't it?"

"I agree." Jo was already drifting out of the room. "Where's the third room that's available?"

"If we go back into the rear hallway and turn left, it will be on your right."

Jo headed that way as I followed. As she went, she said, "The two chapel rooms are pretty, but a room at the back of the building will be nice and quiet, since it doesn't face the street."

Jo easily found the correct door and walked inside the room. Instead of stained glass, the windows were plain, but they were bigger and let in a lot more sunshine. The time-darkened floorboards were covered with a faded old rug I had found in the basement.

"Oh, yes. This room is the one I want! So bright and airy." Jo raised her arms and turned in a circle. "And all that nature outside to greet me in the morning."

I had to admit the view was pretty. There was a dilapidated detached garage at one side of the backyard, but the grass lawn was edged by overgrown bushes and a low stone wall that was covered in a soft green layer of moss. Behind the wall was a small forested area of Douglas firs, with squat magnolia trees peppered among them.

"How much?" Jo asked.

I tentatively said how much I was asking for each month in rent, and when Jo responded with an enthusiastic, "Perfect!" I realized I might have underestimated the rental market in Foxfire Haven, Washington. Still, that was one room rented. Only two to go, and then I'd have enough income to get the ancient heating system repaired.

"I just have one question, though," Jo said. She walked slowly, putting one foot directly in front of the other like a tightrope walker. "Why is the floor slanted?"

When I didn't answer immediately, Jo turned to me. "It's not a deal-breaker," she reassured me. "It's really not all that noticeable."

"That's not why I'm hesitating." I took in a deep breath, then said in a rush, "This was the embalming room. I put the rug down because there's a drain in the floor. The floor is sloped toward the drain."

Jo's eyes widened. She looked shocked, then horrified. Then, to my surprise, she started to laugh. "Of course it was the embalming room. Just my luck! My manifesting magic has backfired again." She had put the intention she'd written inside her purse, but she pulled it out again. "I wrote that the room would be a relaxing, laid-back space. I'm literally going to be laid back on my sloping bed."

"Do you want one of the other rooms instead?" I asked.

"No. This one is my favorite, as long as I don't think about the work that went on in here. By the way, your classified ad will run in tomorrow's edition of the newspaper, so hopefully, you'll fill these other two rooms pretty quickly. I'm not good at living alone, so I'm looking forward to having a full house of roommates."

I just nodded in response. I had been living on my own quite happily before my unexpected return to Foxfire Haven, and unlike Jo, I wasn't looking forward to having roommates. I was used to being independent, and I knew getting used to having three other people living with me was going to take some time.

With other people in the house, I'd have to be mindful of things like not making too much noise late at night or using up all the hot water with a long shower.

I wasn't going to be alone anymore. To most people, that would sound like heaven. To me, it sounded like a punishment.

"How did you get into the kitchen, anyway?" I asked as I led the way out of the embalming room.

Jo's room, I corrected myself.

"Oh, your front door was wide open. I thought you did that so potential renters could come on in and look around."

I frowned. "I didn't open it. I wonder how—"

My wondering would have to wait. A horrible yowl came from outside, followed by a clattering sound.

I hustled toward the front door, which was open, just as Jo had said. A gigantic black cat was standing on the top step of the front porch, its gaze fixed on something directly in front of it.

As soon as I stepped over the threshold, I saw what the cat was focused on, even as it let out a hiss. A wicker basket that had been sitting on the railing had landed upside down on the porch, and it moved slightly. Distressed hoots and frantic flapping sounds came from inside it.

I stepped in front of the basket and made a shooing motion at the cat. "Get away from my familiar, right now!"

TWO

Jo LUNGED PAST ME, stomping toward the cat. It stopped its hissing but stared her down with narrowed green eyes. "Bad cat!" With every word Jo spoke, she stomped a foot. The porch shuddered from the force. "Go away, right now!"

Slowly, the cat turned and sauntered down the front stairs. When it reached the ground, it paused long enough to give Jo and me a look that clearly said it was merely tolerating us. It wasn't going to be scared away by a couple of humans.

While Jo stood guard, I hurried to the basket and lifted it. Perkins, my familiar, was still hooting and flapping his brown-and-cream-colored wings.

"You're safe, Perky," I said soothingly.

Perkins gave me a long-suffering look, but he did, at least, calm down.

"I know it doesn't feel like home yet, but it will." At least, that was what I kept telling myself.

"That is the cutest little owl I have ever seen." Jo bent at the waist and stroked Perkins's head with one finger. He blinked his wide yellow eyes rapidly and clicked his beak. Jo yanked her hand back. "Oh, sorry!"

"That means he likes you," I said. "Trust me, you'd know it if Perkins didn't want you to pet him."

"I assumed you're a witch, but I've never seen an older witch with a baby familiar. I thought most of us bonded with our animals in adolescence."

"Perkins and I met when I was thirteen. He's not a baby. He's a burrowing owl. This is as big as they get." At just eight inches tall, Perkins was never going to be as fierce as some of the other familiars I had seen. My best friend in high school had been escorted everywhere by a bobcat.

"My familiar is a pelican." Jo sounded almost embarrassed as she said it. "He's gigantic, but I promise, he's well-behaved. Plus, he prefers to do his own fishing, so you don't have to worry about me trying to feed him here."

"Maybe he can be Perky's bodyguard," I suggested. I scooped Perkins up with one hand, and he instantly nestled against my blue T-shirt. Familiars lived unusually long lives, often outlasting the witches they were bonded with. My diminutive owl had been in my care for forty years.

Though, sometimes, I felt like he was the one taking care of me, especially lately.

"This isn't the first time that cat has tried to corner Perkins," I continued. "I think it belongs to the man who lives three doors down, so I'll go have a talk with him later."

"Good luck. Oh, and is there a rental agreement I need to sign?"

I felt my cheeks warm. "That would be the proper thing to do," I admitted. "Honestly, though, I was so busy thinking about needing the income that I forgot about that part. I'll, uh, put something together."

Jo waved a hand. "No rush. I just agreed to rent a former embalming room in a haunted funeral home. I'm not worried about someone else swooping in and getting the room."

The whole living situation sounded ridiculous when Jo put it that way, and I had to laugh. "Maybe you should start writing about your ideal roommates," I suggested.

Jo tapped a long finger against her chin. "That's a great idea. I'll work on that during my lunch break today. Ideal roommates and ideal familiars. We don't want another cat-versus-owl situation."

"Any help you can give me in this process is appreciated."

"What are roommates for?" Jo waved again, this time in farewell. "I'll call you when I figure out what day I can move in. See you soon, Hazel!"

I stayed on the front porch and watched as Jo got into her small sedan and drove away. Once the car had disappeared around the bend in the road, I let my gaze rove over the houses ranged along the street. My yard was the most expansive, probably because no one had wanted to build a house too close to a funeral home.

The homes were rather large, but older and slightly shabby. They had a lived-in and much-loved look to them. I hoped I would eventually find my new neighborhood charming. At the moment, though, I was still getting used to the idea that I'd come slinking back to my hometown with my tail between my legs.

Proverbial tail, of course. Witches didn't have tails.

I took Perkins into the kitchen and put him in a nest made from strips of old flannel pajamas. I'd piled the strips in a wicker basket and set it right next to the radiator in the kitchen.

Unfortunately, the radiator only warmed the air a few degrees, and it would only get worse as we moved into fall. Getting the heating system fixed was my top priority, since I didn't think my renters would appreciate freezing to death in their beds.

Once Perkins was settled into his nest, I grabbed my keys and left the house, still wondering how the front door had wound up gaping open in the first place.

I set out with the intention to be polite but firm with my neighbor, but my anger grew as I walked toward the house that I was fairly certain the cat lived in. This was the third time the cat had cornered Perkins, and even though it had been years since I'd lived in Foxfire Haven, I was sure there were still laws about keeping the peace between familiars.

So, by the time my feet hit the driveway leading to a two-story house painted a gloomy shade of gray, I was stomping with as much force as Jo had been just minutes earlier.

Then, my fist tried to equal the fervor of my feet as I pounded on the door.

It was almost like the man who answered the door had known I was coming, because he already looked annoyed as he said, "You're the lady living in the funeral home."

"Former funeral home," I corrected. "Where your familiar just tried to kill mine."

"Jazz isn't a familiar. He's just a cat."

"Well, your cat just tried to kill my owl!"

The man's broad shoulders hitched upward, and he narrowed his ice-blue eyes. He looked like the hero in an old Western about to square off with the villain. A perfectly timed breeze even lifted his silver hair off his forehead, making the whole moment more dramatic. "Then you should keep a better eye on your owl. Shouldn't he be in a cage or up a tree, or something?"

I crossed my arms. My head only came up to the man's shoulder, so I tried to look as menacing as I could despite having to crane my head upward to meet his gaze. "I would never make my familiar live in a cage! And he's a burrowing owl, which means he digs holes in the ground. That's why he wasn't up a tree any of the three times your cat tried to kill him!"

The man slowly raised one eyebrow. "Oh, it's three times now, is it? I thought it was just once."

"I was willing to let it go the first two times. I didn't want to be the kind of neighbor who moves in and immediately starts complaining."

"Yet here you are."

I didn't realize my hands had curled into fists until I felt the stab of my housekey digging into one palm. There were several choice words I wanted to call the man, but I reminded myself to be polite. Yelling and name-calling weren't going to make his cat behave.

But magic could.

I instantly banished the thought from my mind. That simply wasn't an option for me at the moment.

Instead, I forced myself to uncurl my hands and said slowly, "Please see to it that your cat doesn't bother my owl again."

Without waiting for the man to respond, I turned and left. The sight of his cat darting up a tree only made me angrier.

Once I was home again, I channeled all of my angst into scrubbing the floor in the kitchen. The leaky sink, I decided, was work for a plumber.

The classified ad was in the newspaper the next day, just as Jo had promised.

But no one called that day, or the day after that.

When it had been forty-eight hours without a single bite for the remaining two rooms, I printed off some flyers and set out for town so I could hang them on any telephone pole or bulletin board with available space.

Along the way, I figured, maybe I could find a business with a part-time position available. I was determined to get that heating system fixed, one way or another.

Downtown Foxfire Haven was only half a mile from the funeral home, and since some early-morning drizzle had died down, I decided to walk.

The street I lived on ended at the two-lane road that led through downtown—where its name changed to the unoriginal Main Street—so I turned right onto it and soon found myself passing buildings that dated as far back as the late eighteen hundreds. I remembered the white three-story hotel from my childhood, but the little market that had once been next to it now had a sign out front, proclaiming it was a food hall.

The Foxfire Haven Town Hall stood at the center of downtown. For more than a hundred years, the town hall had been where citizens gathered for everything from celebrations to—allegedly—a group effort to hex a traveling salesman who had sold faulty vacuum cleaners to a lot of locals. I was pretty sure that one was just a local legend, but I knew the community bulletin board just inside the front doors was real.

The grand brick building topped by a white cupola sat back from the road, with a small park in front of it that was full of benches, each bearing a brass memorial plaque for some long-gone pillar of the community.

No one was in the foyer when I went inside, and I hastily tacked my flyer to the board and hurried back out to the street. At some point, I had to stop avoiding people and dive into my new life.

And that point, I decided, was right then and there. Across the street, I spotted the Sit a Spell Tavern. I had never been inside it, since I had been too young to go there when I lived in the town before. At the moment, the Tudor-style half-timber building and sagging slate roof looked comforting, somehow, like a cozy little spot where I could step out of my comfort zone without too much hassle.

When I walked inside the tavern, I paused for a moment to let my eyes adjust to the low lighting. There was a long bar along the left wall, but since it wasn't quite noon, no one was sitting at it yet.

There were, however, a few patrons sitting at the round tables in the middle of the room or in the dark booths along the right-hand side. At the back, someone was lazily throwing darts at a board.

"Hey, honey, sit anywhere you like," a woman called. I looked over to see the bartender, who was already grabbing a menu to bring me.

Quickly, I moved toward her. "I was just wondering if there's anywhere I can post a flyer?"

"Oh, sure. The board's over there." The woman jerked her head toward the door. I had walked right past the bulletin board.

As I was pinning a flyer to the board, I heard someone walk up behind me. The person was standing far too close, but before I could scoot away, I heard a man drawl, "*Rooms to rent. Call Hazel Underwood*...Huh. So you're related to Grant."

I turned to see a lanky older man with dark hair that hung limply around his ears. He was looking at me with a mixture of curiosity and dislike.

"He was my uncle," I confirmed.

"So you're living out at that funeral home."

"Yes. I inherited it from him. And, as you see, I'm looking to rent out a few of the rooms."

"I can't imagine anyone will want to take you up on that. At least, not anyone who knows about Grant Underwood."

THRee

"WHAT ARE YOU SAYING?" I began to take a step toward the man, then reminded myself that I was, in fact, trying to back away from him. "Did you have a problem with my uncle?"

"Sure. Lots of us did." The man shifted so his feet were planted firmly, and he crossed his arms. Dark eyes glittered underneath his bushy graying eyebrows.

He clearly wanted me to ask why, so I complied, keeping my tone as neutral as possible. Uncle Grant hadn't been someone I'd known very well, but I had never heard a bad word about him. Growing up, I had always thought of him as a kind, funny man who always had a silly joke at the ready.

"Grant Underwood spent too much time with all those dead bodies, and it finally got to him," the man said, drawing the words out with relish. "He got to the point where he didn't know how to talk to all us living folk anymore."

I shook my head. "That's ridiculous."

"Is it? You can ask other people around this town, and they'll say the same thing. He got weird, and no one wanted to be around him anymore. He was creepy."

You're creepy, I wanted to retort.

Luckily, before I could say anything I might regret, the bartender came to my rescue. "Roscoe Palladano, you hush! You're the one always going on about showing respect for the dead, and here you are, bad-mouthing this woman's family." She had been listening to our conversation from her spot behind the bar, but she was making her way toward us, a stern look on her face.

Roscoe whirled around and glared at the woman. "I pay you to pour beers, not to lecture me!"

"Go sit down and mind your own business, Roscoe, or I won't be pouring you anything today." The woman was petite, but she seemed twice the size of Roscoe as he shrank back. Her long white hair was twisted up into a knot on top of her head, and her hands were firmly planted on her hips. She reminded me so much of my grandmother in that moment I almost laughed out loud.

Roscoe slunk back to his seat at one of the booths, muttering something about lousy bartenders as he went.

"Thanks," I said, turning my attention to the bartender once Roscoe was a safe distance away.

"Sorry about that. Roscoe is rude to everyone. Apparently, he's even more rude to newcomers."

"I grew up here," I said, as if that should have gained me membership into some kind of club for locals who wouldn't get harassed by people like Roscoe.

"I'm guessing it's been a long time since you lived here. I came to Foxfire Haven almost thirty years ago, and I've never seen you around. And in a town this size, it's tough not to get noticed."

"Clearly." I waved vaguely in Roscoe's direction. He was still muttering but quietly enough that I couldn't make out the words. "I just moved back a few weeks ago."

The woman's eyes flicked to the bulletin board, which was behind me. "You're the one living at the funeral home."

I laughed softly. "Talk about getting noticed."

"Everyone has been talking about you. When an abandoned funeral home suddenly has someone living in it, and that someone seems to be avoiding people, the town is going to gossip. Working here, I get to hear all the speculation about who you are, and why you want to live in a funeral home."

"Former funeral home."

"I'm Valerian Bellamy, and I might be your new room-mate." Valerian nodded. "I saw the classified ad, but I haven't managed to give you a call yet. I'm looking to downsize, and this might be a good living situation for me."

"Anyone who stands up for me and my family would be a welcome addition. I'm Hazel. Grant was my uncle."

"I didn't know him. Not really. He used to come to the tavern occasionally, but that was years ago. I'm sure he wasn't as weird as Roscoe is claiming, though. He likes to rile people up. Come on over to the bar and have a seat. This place will be quiet until noon, so you can fill me in on this room I'm going to be renting."

Soon, I was perched on a stool in the middle of the long mahogany bar, with a diet soda in front of me. Valerian had returned to her spot behind the bar, where shelves held the types of liquor bottles I was used to see-ing. Alongside them, though, were various earthenware jugs and glass bottles containing unknown liquids.

I pointed toward a group of squat jugs with corks shoved into their spouts. "Do you serve homemade alcohol here?"

Valerian looked surprised by my question, and she laughed. "You really haven't lived here in a long time. And, I'm guessing, wherever you were living until a few weeks ago wasn't a magical town."

"I was living in San Francisco." There were small towns across the country where witches and other magical or supernatural creatures could live without needing to hide their abilities. I knew from my decades in San Francisco that people in the mundane world told stories about the magical towns, but no one seemed to believe them. The idea that witches and other supernatural beings existed seemed too strange for most people, so they passed off the rumors as silly superstitions about small-town folks.

And, of course, all those magical small-town folks were perfectly happy to nod and say of course, they must be nothing more than silly rumors.

"Those bottles are all various potions," Valerian explained. "I brewed some of them myself, but I also have suppliers. That green bottle is my most popular potion, because it's a luck elixir. Someone having a bad day will pop in here for my specialty drink, a Good Mojo Martini. Does it actually make them luckier? Maybe. What I know for sure is that the drink makes them feel better after a bad day."

I eyed the lucky elixir. "Maybe that's what I need. Unless you have a potion that will magically fix the heating system in the funeral home."

"There's only one thing that will magically fix that, and that's money." Valerian gave a sharp nod. "I've got a friend who knows how to work on those old systems, and she'll give you a good deal. After all, she wouldn't want me to be a human icicle in my new home. Speaking of which, tell me about the living situation at this place."

I filled Valerian in on the funeral home, including that the two available bedrooms had once been used to host funerals. She seemed undaunted by that idea, but her face fell when I broke the news that there was currently only one shower for all four of us to share.

"The bathrooms that were installed for funeral attendees only have toilets and sinks," I explained. "The one tub and shower in the house are in the private suite where I'm living, though that bathroom is easy to access, since it has its own door off the back hallway. But, before you despair, know that I'm planning to change that as soon as I can. Once the heating is repaired, I'm going to save up money to redo the bathrooms."

Valerian pursed her lips. "I've got somebody who can help with that, too, if you haven't found anyone yet."

"I'll gladly take your recommendations, especially if it's another friend who will give me a deal because they don't want to think about you waiting in line to shower."

"It's my ex-brother-in-law, actually," Valerian said. She got a thoughtful look on her face. "As a matter of fact, he might be tempted to charge me more because I used to be married to his brother. I'll give you his info, and you can leave my name out of the conversation."

"I'll pretend I've never met you." I paused, feeling suddenly awkward. "Valerian, um, speaking of money, I'm also looking for some part-time work."

Why am I embarrassed about needing a job?

"We don't have any openings here at the tavern," Valerian said, "unless you can do beer and liquor delivery for us. Our usual delivery guy, Steve, hasn't shown up for two weeks, and no one can track him down. He probably went on another road trip without telling anyone. Someone needs to head over to Stanton to pick up our restock. If we run out of beer, Roscoe will be even more cantankerous!"

"Why don't you ask the distributor to deliver your order to you?"

Valerian gave me a lopsided smile. "Again, you're really showing how long it's been since you've lived here, or in any magical town. Remember, we like keeping to ourselves. We don't need non-magical people taking stories back to their towns about strange potions behind the bar or witches working charms to make the town hall's grass grow better."

"Of course. It's much better to go out and collect anything from the outside world, rather than the outside world coming to us." I sighed. "I was eighteen when I left this town, and now that I'm back, I feel like I'm having to relearn everything I ever knew about living in Foxfire Haven. Plus, I have to start my social life from scratch. I've only run into two people I used to know, but that's no surprise. I was kind of an awkward kid, so I didn't have a lot of friends, and the rest of my family moved away years ago."

"Don't worry. You'll make lots of friends this time around, and everything about life in a magical town will come back to you. Just be prepared for a lot of folks to ask you about living in a big city. Most of us have only ever lived in tiny towns like this one, and we consider people like you to be great adventurers."

"I'm not nearly as exciting as you think I am," I said, but I could feel the smile tugging at my lips. Back when I left Foxfire Haven, people like me had been looked down on for leaving the tight-knit magical community. It was nice to know perceptions had changed in the years since then. "I think living in the Taylor Brothers Funeral Home is far more of an adventure."

As if to emphasize my point, there was a bang behind me. I swiveled on my bar stool to see the front door of the tavern wide open. A huge form was framed in the doorway, and the sunshine streaming into the tavern threw the figure's features into shadow.

The newcomer lumbered in my direction, and I instinctively shrank back against the bar as I got my first good look at the honey-colored fur, bared teeth, and massive hands.

A Bigfoot had just walked into the tavern, and he was heading straight toward me.

Four

I WAS FROZEN ON my barstool as the Bigfoot moved closer. I'd heard of these creatures, and when I was a teenager, I had even caught a glimpse of one while driving home from the movies one night.

Seeing a Bigfoot up close was an entirely different experience. This one was at least seven feet tall, and he looked strong enough to tear me in half.

My body was still, but my mind was racing. *Should I get up and run? Should I try to climb over the bar and hide behind it? Or,* I thought wildly, *if I just stay perfectly still, maybe the Bigfoot won't notice me.*

Even as I told myself that was a silly idea, the creature veered slightly to one side, eventually coming to rest on the stool at the far end of the bar. As I gaped at the sight, I saw Valerian sweep up to him with a glass and a bottle of brown liquid. In a flash, the Bigfoot had a drink in front of him.

I was still staring when Valerian returned to me and put a gentle hand on my arm. "Hey," she said under her breath. "Try not to look. He doesn't like attention."

With an effort, I tore my eyes away. It was only then I realized my hands were shaking. "I thought he was going to kill me."

"Bigfoots don't attack humans," Valerian said. "Another piece of magical life you've probably forgotten. But, after years off in a big city, I can understand how seeing him is a bit of a shock."

"I can't believe one of your customers is a Bigfoot."

"Barry has been in here every day for weeks now. He's sulking about something. I haven't heard him say more than ten words, and four of those were his drink order. He drinks our most expensive single-malt whisky and nothing else."

"Maybe he and I can sit and sulk together," I mumbled, risking another glance in Barry's direction. He was slowly turning the glass with his massive fingers, staring at the bottles on the shelves in front of him. I wouldn't have thought a Bigfoot could look wistful, but Barry was pulling it off.

"Why are *you* sulking?" Valerian asked.

Oops. "Oh, you know," I hedged. "I need money and a part-time job, and I have to make repairs to the funeral home, and I'm having to relearn everything about living in this town. It's a lot."

"I'll help you get your bearings again," Valerian promised. "It will be easier after I move in. When can I come see the place? I should probably check it out before I commit."

Valerian and I made plans for her to get the same tour Jo had, and then I thanked her again for coming to my defense with Roscoe. I stole one last glance at Barry before heading out.

Just as I was stepping over the threshold of the tavern, my electrician, Archer, was walking up to the door. His thinning brown hair always stuck up in all directions, and that paired with his wide blue eyes made him look like he'd just gotten electrocuted while on the job.

"Hazel, hi. I stopped by this morning, but you were out, so I'll come back tomorrow. I finally got that part I need for the back-porch light."

"Great. Thanks." *And that's another bill I'm going to have to pay soon, too.* With that in mind, I took in a deep breath, squared my shoulders, and turned left on the sidewalk. I was going to stop into every store I passed until I found someone hiring.

I reached the end of the small downtown stretch of Foxfire Haven without finding a single store on the tavern side of the street that was hiring. I gazed at the row of stores and restaurants along the other side of the street, telling myself I should work my way through them, but I was feeling too dispirited at the moment to go through with it.

Instead, I continued walking in the same direction. Downtown soon gave way to a few houses and some vacant lots, but I knew a five-minute walk would bring me to the Growing Power Garden Store. I wanted a few flowers for the bare planters on my front porch, and even if I wasn't ready to buy them right then and there, I figured looking couldn't hurt.

I was browsing a collection of pink and yellow pansies when a woman bustled up to me. Her green T-shirt, which had the garden store's logo on it, was streaked with dirt, and wisps of hair were escaping the blue scarf tied around her head. "Can I help you?" she asked.

"I was just looking for some flowers," I said. Then, before I could chicken out, I added, "And I wanted to ask if you have any job openings."

The woman gazed at me for so long I began to feel uncomfortable. Finally, she asked, "Are you a green witch?"

"No."

"A garden witch?"

"No."

"A grow witch?"

I wanted to answer that all of those sounded like the same thing, but instead, I shook my head.

"What kind of a witch are you, then?"

"I'm a spreadsheet witch."

The woman stared at me blankly. Clearly, my joke hadn't landed. "I worked in an accounting office for twenty years," I explained.

"Yuck. No wonder you want something new. Before that, though, what kind of magic was your specialty?"

"Honestly, my ability was always in planning and organization. Having the right thing just when it's needed, planning trips with perfect timing, knowing exactly how much food to buy for a party, that sort of thing. Those skills served me well in an office setting."

The woman's expression relaxed, and she gave me a smile that showed off her round cheeks. "Ah-ha! You're what I like to call a mom witch. Always prepared, and always ready with the right words of wisdom or cup of tea for the situation. Highly intuitive."

Mom witch. I wanted to roll my eyes at the concept, because I wasn't a very good mom or a very good witch.

"With those kinds of skills, you should be able to find a job pretty easily," the woman continued. Before I could tell her that was definitely not the case, she continued, "You're new here. I haven't seen you before."

"I grew up here, but I went to college in California. I wound up meeting a non-magical guy there, and we moved to San Francisco after graduation."

"Did he know?"

I shrugged. "I told him I was a witch, but he always seemed to think I was like a child playing dress-up. It was one of the many reasons we got divorced."

"Ah, a divorce. That explains why you've come back to Foxfire Haven."

I shook my head. "No. He and I got divorced years ago. He's been married and divorced twice since we split up. I thought I'd stay in San Francisco for the rest of my life, but it became clear I needed a fresh start somewhere else."

Something red moved into my field of vision, and I looked to see a man about eighteen inches tall walking past, carrying a tray of seedlings. He had a long white beard, and the red I had spotted was the conical hat that sat right on the top of his head. He, too, was wearing a green T-shirt emblazoned with the store's logo.

After he had passed from view, I said, "I've heard of garden gnomes, but I didn't know there were real ones."

The woman snorted out a laugh and quickly covered her mouth with one hand. Once she had herself under control, she said, "Don't let him hear you calling him that! He says garden gnomes are just statues. He's a living gnome who just so happens to work at a gardening store."

"How did I live here for the first eighteen years of my life without knowing there are real gnomes in the world?"

"He's the only one I've ever met. Gnorris says there are a lot of them on the east coast."

A Bigfoot and a gnome in one day. I wonder what's next?

"Anyway," the woman continued, "good luck with your job search. I'm Petunia Cornwell. Yes, Petunia. My mom was a garden witch, and she rightly figured I would be, too. You holler if you need anything as you get settled into your new life here. Oh, and are you buying some flowers, or not?"

I glanced at the gorgeous pansies, then sighed. "I walked here, but I'll be back with my car to get some things." *If I have money left over after getting the funeral home fixed up*, I added silently. Getting the heating and electrical work taken care of had to take priority over planting flowers.

As I walked home, I thought about my need to get some income rolling in. Jo and Valerian renting rooms was a great start, but I would still need more. I had a fair amount of money in my savings account, but it wouldn't last forever.

Every funeral home needed a hearse, I knew. I remembered Uncle Grant rolling up to our house in his when I was a kid. My big brother would always run out to the driveway and press his face against the glass in the back, looking for a coffin. He was always disappointed not to find one.

I, on the other hand, would groan every time that hearse pulled up, worried the other kids in the neighborhood would spot it and make fun of me.

Now that I was grown up and in need of some money, I was quickly gaining a whole new respect for the hearse. I'd seen several vintage hearses around San Francisco, fully restored and driven by people who liked the novelty of it. Usually, the drivers wore all black and put on what I thought was far too much black eyeliner.

If there was still a hearse inside the old garage, I knew I could easily sell it to someone in the mundane world, and I could probably get a good chunk of cash for it.

When I got home, I headed directly for the kitchen and grabbed a keyring hanging from a hook just inside the back door. I was soon in the backyard, where the wooden garage stood forlornly. The peeling paint on the clapboard building had once been a bright yellow, perhaps, but it had faded to a dull cream.

The wide double garage doors had rusted handles and an equally rusted lock. I was surprised when I walked up to the doors and found the lock unlatched. When I had first arrived in Foxfire Haven, I had made a thorough sweep of the property, and I was almost certain the doors had been locked. It was the only reason I hadn't gone inside the garage yet. I knew the key must be among the many on the old ring that was now in my hand, but I hadn't yet gone through all the keys to find the right one.

Still, the unlocked doors saved me from having to try one key after another.

The doors had sagged over time, so instead of pulling them open with ease, I had to put in some effort to drag them over the concrete drive that led to the garage. The hinges squealed in protest, and several creaks warned that some of the boards weren't going to hold for much longer.

A musty, rotten smell wafted out from the shadows of the garage, and I wrinkled my nose. There was a grimy paned window along one side of the garage, sitting above a long workbench. Potted plants had been put there years ago, and dead leaves still clung stubbornly to the stalks.

"No wonder it stinks," I muttered as I stepped inside and searched for a light switch. As I had hoped, there was a hearse parked right in front of me, but dirty canvas tarps were covering it, so I couldn't tell what kind of shape it was in.

I found the light switch, but nothing happened when I flicked it on. With a shrug, I moved forward and grabbed the nearest tarp. I coughed as it slid off the back of the black hearse, sending up a massive cloud of dust.

Quickly, I jumped backward, out of the doors and into the fresh air outside. The tarp had landed in a heap to one side of the hearse, and as the dust settled, I saw something else on the ground, just underneath the rear bumper. It was in the shadow of the hearse, and all I could make out was what looked like a bundle of dirty fabric.

I stepped forward, crouched down, and peered at the pile. The fabric was khaki-colored but covered in dark streaks. A metallic glint caught my eye, and I saw a gold watch. The fabric was a shirt, and the watch was secured to the wrist of someone who was very much dead.

Five

THERE'S A BODY IN my garage.

I wasn't sure how long I stood there, too shocked to move. Eventually, a little voice in my mind told me I needed to get moving and call the police.

My cell phone was in the kitchen, next to my purse, where I'd dropped it onto the counter after getting home. I backed away from the garage, feeling unnerved at the idea of turning my back on the body. It wasn't until I reached the back-porch steps that I pivoted and fled up them, shutting and locking the kitchen door behind me with force.

"What do you think is going to happen?" I asked myself. "It's not going to get up and follow you inside."

That cleared my head a bit, and I picked up my phone and dialed nine-one-one. It was only as I selected the final number that I remembered Foxfire Haven didn't have that emergency system. The town was too small for something like that.

I needed to call the police directly.

Constables, I reminded myself. For some reason, magical towns usually referred to their police as constables.

I had the correct name, and that just left me needing the correct number.

I thought back to my childhood, when we'd had a telephone book to look up contact information. I hadn't seen one at the funeral home, not even in the inevitable junk drawer in the kitchen. Maybe I needed to go online to search for the number.

A feeling of panic began to rise in my chest, and I stopped to take a deep breath. *It's not like the dead person is in a hurry,* I reminded myself. There was no reason to feel rushed.

As I was thinking that, my eyes were roving across the kitchen, and I spotted a small sheet of paper stuck to the front of the fridge with a magnet that was shaped like a coffin. The faded handwriting on the paper neatly noted the phone numbers for the constables, the hospital, and other people who might be needed in an emergency. One of them had the ominous title of *Magical Corrections*.

The numbers had been right there the whole time, but I'd been in such a panic that I had entirely forgotten. I wasted no time calling the number for the Foxfire Haven Constables, and a woman answered the phone.

"Is this an immediate emergency?" she asked, sounding much calmer than I did.

"No," I admitted.

"Is this related to a magical incident?"

"I don't think so."

"Please state the situation and the address."

"I'm at the Taylor Brothers Funeral Home, and there is a body under the hearse."

There was a short pause. "You mean in the hearse?"

"I mean underneath."

The woman responded in a tone that indicated she was putting effort into maintaining her patient demeanor. "Bodies are expected in hearses. How is this a matter for the constables?"

I shut my eyes and took a deep breath. Clearly, this was going to require a little more explanation. "The funeral home has been closed for the past six years. There shouldn't be any bodies here anymore. However, when I went into the garage just now, I found a body shoved under the back bumper of the old hearse. Either someone crawled into my garage and died, or someone stashed the body there. I would like the constables to come out and investigate." I stopped, then added, "I would also like them to remove the body."

The woman's voice had returned to its calm, business-like tone when she spoke again. "I see. Two constables should arrive at your funeral home in the next fifteen minutes. Thank you, and have a nice day."

The woman ended the call, and I dropped my phone onto the kitchen counter with a clatter. "Yeah, I'm having such a nice day."

I checked my watch and noted the time. Fifteen minutes. I could make it that long.

Behind me, I heard a quiet hooting, and I turned to see Perkins sitting on a shelf above the grimy gas stove. "I know it will be okay," I told him.

He hooted again and gave his body a shake, puffing out his feathers and partially extending his wings so he looked bigger. In response, I puffed out my chest and lifted my arms, like I was showing off my biceps. "I'm strong, and I'm brave." Perkins always seemed to know when I needed a reminder that I was stronger than I realized, and over the years, I'd learned that when he puffed up his feathers, he was telling me just that.

What am I supposed to do now? It would feel disrespectful to simply go about my business, I realized. I didn't want to lounge on the couch with a book while there was a dead person in my garage. Still, I had to do something.

And, I thought, something that helped me get out some of the adrenaline still coursing through me would be ideal.

With that in mind, I grabbed a bottle of cleaner and a brush, then got to work scrubbing some stubborn stains on the rug in the dining room. They were dark red, and I had been telling myself since the day I moved in that they were probably just the result of a very messy pasta dinner.

One of the stains was looking lighter by the time my doorbell rang. I got up from my spot on the rug as quickly as I could, then made my way to the front door.

Even as I was unlocking the door, there was a knock. I'd had to wait fifteen minutes, but the constables couldn't wait the one minute it took me to reach the front door. Still, I had to appreciate their sense of urgency in dealing with my unexpected problem.

I had what I hoped was a grateful-but-solemn expression on my face as I opened the door.

And then I saw who it was standing there.

"You'll be happy to know my cat is not accompanying me on this call," my neighbor said.

My cranky, insolent, "the cat is innocent" neighbor crossed his arms and stood up a little straighter, looking down his nose at me. The constable uniform was a crisp gray shirt with black pants, and there was a ring around the silver pentagram on his chest.

He wasn't just a constable. He was the chief constable of Foxfire Haven.

I decided to ignore the cat comment in the interest of keeping things civil. "The body is in the garage, in the backyard," I said simply.

The other constable who had accompanied my neighbor turned and began to head down the porch steps. As he went, he called over his shoulder, "Should I grab the crime scene kit from the car?"

"No." My neighbor was talking to him but still looking at me. "Let's wait and take a look before we make any assumptions."

As the other constable disappeared around the corner of my house, my neighbor narrowed his eyes at me. "You're related to Underwood."

"I inherited this place from my Uncle Grant, yes."

"Come on, then, Underwood. Let's go see this alleged body."

"It is not alleged, and my name is Hazel."

He grunted. "Chief Constable Wyatt Hightower. Nice to formally meet you, Hazel." Wyatt didn't sound like it was at all nice to meet me, formally or not. "It's always good to get to know your neighbors, isn't it?"

I wasn't sure that was true, if my neighbors were going to be like this guy. Wyatt was already following his colleague, so I shut the front door behind me and trailed in his wake. As I walked through the grass, I kept reminding myself to be nice. The guy might be a curmudgeon, but he was also the one who was going to deal with whatever had happened in my garage.

When I reached the backyard, I saw the other constable squatting down just behind the hearse.

"What's it looking like, Callan?" Wyatt called.

"Exactly what was reported." Callan stood. "I'll go grab the crime scene kit."

As he passed by me on his way to the car, Callan gave me a sympathetic look. I wasn't sure if it was because I had a dead person on my hands, or because I was having to deal with Wyatt.

Wyatt's arm shot out as I stepped up next to him, blocking my way. "Stay back. If this is a crime scene, you don't want to contaminate it. Did you touch or move anything when you found him?"

"So it's a man under there?" I bent forward slightly, so I could get a closer look without bumping into Wyatt's arm. "Was he murdered? And, if so, why was he stashed in my garage? How long has he been there? Did this murder happen a long time ago, or recently?"

Wyatt didn't answer any of my questions, but he lowered his arm and turned slowly to stare me down with those blue eyes of his. Suddenly, I felt like I was suspect number one, but his gaze did, at least, get me to stop my rambling. I realized the shock was beginning to wear off, and if I had continued talking, I might have quickly spiraled into panic.

And then, I knew, I would start crying, and there was no way in the world I was ever going to let Wyatt Hightower see me cry.

Callan returned and plunked down what I assumed was the crime scene kit, though to me it looked like an old-fashioned black leather doctor's bag. I had forgotten how archaic some of the practices in a magical town like Foxfire Haven were. Growing up, they had seemed perfectly normal. After all my years living in San Francisco, they seemed like something from a nineteen fifties TV show.

The contents of the bag, at least, looked perfectly modern. Soon, Callan was taking photos with a digital camera while Wyatt scribbled something in a small notebook. I was curious to see how they would handle the whole thing, but I also didn't want to stand there like an interloper, so I asked if either of them wanted something to drink. Wyatt only grunted in answer, but Callan requested a glass of water.

I had locked the kitchen door earlier, so I had to walk around to the front of the house again. Along the way, I only grumbled once about Wyatt and his attitude problem.

No sooner had I stepped into the kitchen than a man with a shimmering, transparent form popped up in front of me. "Oh, those uniforms are so unflattering!"

SIX

My shriek was so loud I half-expected the constables to come running to the back door to find out what was amiss. I clamped one hand over my mouth and the other over my pounding heart.

The ghost threw back his head and laughed. "That was fantastic! I wasn't even trying to scare you."

I lowered the hand that was covering my mouth so Holman could get a full view of my glare. "It's not funny! There's a dead man in the garage! Did you know about this?"

Holman stopped laughing and raised his hands defensively. His light-gray suit was cut in a style that made him look like he should be starring in an old gangster movie. Even his wavy blond hair and pencil mustache had a vintage look. "I did not know, and if I had, I would have informed you. That chief constable is a handsome fella, isn't he? Too bad that uniform makes him look so stuffy."

"It's not the uniform making him look like that. Wyatt Hightower is a cranky old man." I pulled two glasses out of the cabinet, then plunked them down onto the countertop with force.

"Hightower? Oh, his family has been in this town for ages." Holman raised a finger and pretended to add up numbers. "It must have been his great-granddaddy that I prepared for burial back in thirty-one. The guy was hit with a curse while trying to break up a ring of liquor smugglers one town over. No one knew they had a powerful witch working with them."

"How awful." I glanced in the direction of the back door. "Wyatt's family has been in law enforcement for generations, then."

"Apparently. The uniforms weren't great back then, either." Holman made a *tsk* noise. "I've always thought people would be better about obeying the law if our constables dressed with a little more panache. But, they never asked for my fashion advice."

"No, I can't imagine many people in Foxfire Haven were asking the funeral home director for fashion tips."

Holman shrugged, the padding in the shoulders of his suit making the gesture especially dramatic. "I made the dead look fantastic, but people never stopped to think about how I could transform the living. Anyway, I just wanted to drop in to pass along my thoughts about those unfortunate uniforms."

"Thank you, Holman," I said, smiling despite the scene happening in my garage at that moment. "Your disapproval has been noted. By the way, I've got some potential roommates coming over in the next few days. You may have seen Jo when she was here a couple days ago. Please, no matter how badly someone is dressed, be kind. I need rent money to get this place looking nice again."

"Fine. I'll wait until after they've paid the first month's rent before I make any comments."

Holman faded away, and I glanced down at my own outfit, surprised he hadn't weighed in on my pink-and-white flowered blouse and faded jeans. Maybe I looked better than I had realized, because Holman wouldn't have hesitated to tell me if he thought I was a fashion disaster.

I took two glasses of water to the backyard, figuring Wyatt's grunt might have been his version of "yes, please," and saw that the two constables were placing numbered markers in various places.

"I hope you're finding some helpful evidence," I commented as I put the glasses on the ground next to the crime scene bag.

Wyatt grunted again in answer. It was, apparently, his default noise.

"We're going to have to move the hearse," Callan said. "After we move the body, of course. The coroner is on her way."

I nodded. "Sure. Do whatever you need to do."

I felt something wet against my cheek. Was I crying? No, I realized. It was beginning to drizzle. I had been used to a fair amount of rain in San Francisco, but that city had nothing on the state of Washington.

The weather seemed to be my cue to head inside, where I continued my attack on the hopefully-just-pasta-sauce stains in the dining room. After that, I threw in a load of laundry, gave the empty chapels-turned-bedrooms another sweep so they would look nice when Valerian came by, and began a deep clean of the small pantry off the kitchen.

The entire time, I only looked out the back windows once. The coroner had arrived, as well as three more constables. I went out front to check the mail, and I was happy to see the hearse lumbering slowly down the driveway, toward the street. The old thing still ran, which meant I'd be able to get a decent amount of money for it.

Though why it was being driven away was beyond me. Not wanting to see whatever was happening with the body, though, I opted to wait and ask once things were finally wrapped up.

It wasn't until four o'clock in the afternoon, more than three hours after I had called the constables, that Wyatt came to the door and informed me they were finished.

"I saw the hearse heading out," I said. "Did Callan take it for a joyride?"

I was pretty sure Wyatt almost smiled at my joke. "We had to move it to look for evidence on the floor near the victim. Callan put in a new battery and took it to our warehouse to give it another thorough search, and you'll get it back when the investigation is finished."

"Can I go inside the garage now, or do I need to steer clear?"

"Maybe leave it be for a couple days. We were thorough, but depending on what the coroner finds in the autopsy, we might want to come back for a second look." Wyatt hesitated. "Listen, Underwood. I know you might be feeling pretty unsettled about all this. I don't think you're in danger, though."

I blinked at Wyatt, trying to process what he had just said. "That hadn't even occurred to me. Why would I be in danger?"

"Someone was likely murdered, and the body was stashed inside your garage. You hadn't considered this might be personal?"

I took a step back, wanting to slam the door and go hide under my covers. "I just got to town three weeks ago! I don't think I've made any enemies in that time."

"Relax. I'm not saying it *is* personal. In fact, I don't think it is. My guess is that the funeral home has been vacant for so long someone thought it was a good place to hide a body. No one knew you were going to show up one day and move in. So, what I'm trying to say is, if you had been afraid the killer would come after you next, you can stop worrying."

Except, now that Wyatt had planted that idea in my head, I *was* worried. What was I going to do if someone came after me in the middle of the night? Holman certainly wouldn't be able to help me fight someone off. He would just make snarky comments about the killer's outfit while my life was in the balance.

Maybe it was the look on my face, or maybe it was standard procedure, but Wyatt reached into a pocket and pulled out a business card. "Here. My home number is on this, just in case. Since I'm only three doors down, I can get here quick."

"Thanks," I said. I'd take a curmudgeonly defender any day over none at all.

Once Wyatt had gone, that left me with a quiet house and a crime scene in my backyard. I collapsed onto the couch, feeling overwhelmed and uncertain what to do next.

I must have fallen asleep, because I jumped at the sound of the doorbell and looked out the window to see the afternoon was nearly spent. I glanced at my watch. Six o'clock. Valerian was right on time.

As soon as I opened the door, I knew the news of the murder victim in my backyard had already spread through town. Or, at any rate, news had made it as far as the tavern. Valerian's eyes were wide, and she was impatiently tapping one hand against her thigh. "Tell me everything," she said in greeting.

"I don't know much," I admitted. "I didn't want to sit and watch while the police were doing their work. If you don't want to rent a room here anymore, I totally understand."

Valerian tilted her head and gave me a long look. "It's not like this is the first dead body to be on this property," she pointed out. "You think I'm going to back out because someone was killed in your garage?"

"Wow. You even know where he was found? News does travel fast."

"I'm a bartender. I hear it all." Valerian stepped forward, and I moved out of her way as she came inside. "Oh, this place looks just like I remember it. Is it still haunted by that old funeral director?"

I snickered. "You really do hear it all, if you know about Holman. Yes, he's still here, but don't let him hear you calling him old!"

Valerian lifted her face toward the ceiling. In a loud voice, she called, "Sorry, Holman! I should have called you a *former* funeral director, not an old one."

"You'll find other things to call him after he shows up to critique your makeup, or your hair, or your outfit."

"I'd heard he just floated at the back of funerals, but that makes him sound like a lousy roommate."

"Holman takes pride in how well he made the deceased look, and he thinks it gives him the right to judge how well we, the living, look. He showed up earlier to complain about the uniforms the constables are wearing these days. By the way, what do you know about Wyatt Hightower?"

"He's very stoic," Valerian answered without hesitation. "I know he was married at one point, but I'm not sure what happened. He keeps to himself, and he rarely visits the tavern. Was he the one running the show today?"

"Yes, and he's a neighbor. We don't get along too well. I was wondering if it was just me he doesn't like, or if he's grumpy with everyone."

"He's more quiet than grumpy, I'd say. Are the available rooms these two here at the front? Oh, wow, I remember this hallway from my great-grandma's funeral. Us kids got in trouble for running up and down it during the viewing."

Valerian didn't need me to guide her. After a quick look inside each of the two former chapels, she pointed at the one on the right-hand side of the hallway. "I'll take this one. The other is where Great-Grammy's funeral was held, and I think it might be strange to sleep in there."

I also showed Valerian around the kitchen and dining area, and her enthusiasm for the place grew as we went. "It's going to be cozy once you have all the rooms rented and we have our belongings here. I like that you're bringing all this life to the place. But my new life here will have to wait just a bit. I'm on my dinner break, so I need to get back to the tavern."

After seeing Valerian out, I went into the kitchen to start on my own dinner, but the doorbell rang again before I could make much headway chopping up broccoli. My first thought was that Valerian had come back for some reason.

My second thought was that the killer had come back.

I was really holding a grudge against Wyatt for putting that idea in my head.

And, unfortunately, he was the one at the front door. *Better him than the killer,* I told myself.

"Our initial assessment has been confirmed," Wyatt said as soon as I opened the door. Without waiting for me to invite him in, he stepped over the threshold and began heading down the hall. He didn't speak again until he found the living room—which had once been the showroom, full of caskets for families to purchase. The living room in the private suite was far too small for myself and three renters, but the old showroom had plenty of space.

Wyatt perched on the edge of a burgundy chair. "This was murder."

"I never doubted it," I said, sinking down onto the couch. "Did you come here just to tell me that?"

"And to ask you some questions. I did some digging into your background this afternoon."

I leaned forward and rested my elbows on my knees. Something about Wyatt's tone had put me on edge. Did he think I was a suspect? I made a go-ahead motion with my hand, but I could see the way it shook. Hopefully, Wyatt hadn't noticed.

Wyatt leaned forward, too, his eyes fixed on mine. "I know about your magical incident in San Francisco."

The room around me seemed to pull out of focus for a moment, and my breath hitched in my chest. "Oh. You talked to my daughter."

seven

"Your daughter and I had a long chat," Wyatt said. The corners of his lips twitched downward. "And I know why you came back to Foxfire Haven."

"I'm not dangerous," I said in a rush.

"Tara also told me the incident wasn't the first time something like that has happened."

"I never hurt anyone." I could hear the pleading in my voice. "And I've definitely never killed anyone with my magic."

Instead of responding, Wyatt simply continued to stare at me. His gaze was so intense I had to fight the urge to squirm or look away. *He thinks I murdered that man with my magic.*

"My magic was never very strong, anyway." I was surprised to hear myself offering up that bit of information. I pressed my lips together and looked away. "Is this your magic? Making people talk?"

There was silence for a few seconds. "I've been a constable for a long time. I'm just good at my job. That's all."

"If I had murdered the guy, I would have left him there in the garage. I wouldn't have called the police. Constables, I mean."

"You were in the mundane world for a long time."

"Since I left for college when I was eighteen."

"And three weeks after your return to Foxfire Haven, you just so happen to stumble on a dead body. Maybe you killed him, but you weren't strong enough to haul the body somewhere to dispose of it. Instead, you called the constables and pretended you discovered the body when you went inside the garage."

Do I need a lawyer? I wondered. Wyatt's theory was wild, and I suspected he didn't really believe it. Still, he seemed to think there was more to the story than I was admitting. I spread my hands, feeling defeated. "Are you arresting me?"

Wyatt stood up, and he towered over me as I shrank back on the couch. "For what?" he asked coolly. "You said you didn't murder anyone. But I will be keeping an eye on you, and your magic."

"I haven't...I'm not a practicing witch anymore."

"Your daughter told me that, too. I'll see myself out."

I sat there for a long time after Wyatt had left. I was embarrassed, angry, and exhausted, and I had no one to brew me a cup of tea and tell me it would all be okay.

As reluctant as I had been feeling about renting out rooms, I suddenly wished I had at least one roommate there by my side. We would say mean things about Wyatt while eating ice cream in our pajamas.

Since that wasn't an option, I headed to the kitchen and bypassed my half-prepared dinner, heading instead for the pantry. I would just have to brew my own cup of tea, and Perkins, I knew, would come perch on my shoulder and rub his soft little head against my ear.

"It's all going to be okay," I told myself.

I slept absolutely terribly that night, despite being so tired. Every sound inside the old funeral home seemed amplified, and I sat up whenever one of the floorboards popped or creaked, thinking the killer had come back for me. Those fears would inevitably make me angrier toward Wyatt, who had planted that idea in my head in the first place.

Not surprisingly, I drank a lot of coffee the next morning.

I was applying moisturizer to my face when Holman appeared beside me. "Please tell me you're going to do more than that," he said. "Those dark circles under your eyes are not doing you any favors."

I glanced at the ghost's reflection in the mirror. "You're not helping."

"I am, though. You want to look your best, especially if there's any chance you're going to see that chief constable again."

I raised an eyebrow. "Why? So I can look nice while he's accusing me of murder?"

"Because he's handsome, and if he's going to be staring you down with those baby blues, then you should at least give him something pretty to look at."

I opened my mouth, ready to give Holman a lecture about things no woman wanted to be told, then decided I just didn't have the energy for it. Instead, I asked, "Did you see anything yesterday? I'm sure you looked at the crime scene. Maybe you recognized the victim?"

Holman shook his head. "I can't go outside, so whatever happened in the garage is a mystery to me, too. I did get a good look at the body through the window as the coroner was loading it up, but it wasn't anyone I remember ever seeing here inside the funeral home."

Of course. Holman would only recognize people who had visited the funeral home.

"It's just another strange thing in the annals of this business," Holman continued. He looked at himself in the mirror and tapped a finger underneath one eye. "I don't think I'm looking my best this morning, either."

"Like you ever have dark circles," I said. "You're dead, remember?"

"You say that like it's a bad thing."

"Anyway, what do you mean about this being another strange thing in the funeral home's history? What else has happened?" I figured Holman might not know who had been killed, but perhaps, he had gleaned other information that was linked to the murder.

"Look, I know Grant is a member of your family," Holman began. "And I always hate speaking ill of the dead."

I had finished my morning routine—with the exception of concealer, which I skipped putting under my eyes just to annoy Holman—and I turned to look at the ghost. "But?"

Holman looked slightly uncomfortable. "Grant seemed to think there was a secret hidden here in the funeral home. He became obsessed with it."

"A secret? What kind of a secret?" I thought back to Roscoe, the man at the tavern who had called my uncle weird. Was this obsession what he had been referring to?

Holman shook his head and sighed. "I wouldn't know. I tried to follow Grant around the house so I could learn more, but he realized what I was doing. He worked a temporary banishing spell, and the next thing I knew, ten years had passed, and Grant was already dead when my banishment ended. This house was empty."

I hadn't even known it was possible to banish a ghost for a finite amount of time. It seemed like a terribly mean thing to do to Holman, though if he kept judging my appearance, I might be tempted to get rid of him for a week or so.

"My uncle was always so nice," I said. "At least, that's how I remember him. I'm sorry to hear he did something so awful to you."

"He and I were never close friends, but we got along okay. It took me by surprise, too. Unfortunately, his ghost doesn't seem to have stuck around, so I can't yell at him."

"Or get answers about the alleged secret hidden here. How bizarre."

The rest of my morning was quiet. Holman had disappeared, and there were no more dead bodies for me to stumble across. I got the wainscoting in the dining room prepped for painting—the dingy white paint was horribly discolored in spots, and its once-glossy sheen had faded—and I was just beginning to think about lunch when the doorbell rang.

"Please don't be Wyatt. Please don't be Wyatt." I repeated the sentence like I was saying a spell as I walked to the front door.

Thankfully, it wasn't the chief constable waiting for me on the doorstep. Instead, it was Archer, the electrician who was helping me get the ancient wiring sorted out.

"I heard about the murder," Archer said after wishing me a good morning.

"Everyone in town already knows, I'm guessing."

"There was a newspaper article about it, so probably." Archer hitched a laden canvas bag higher on his shoulder. "The story says the vic was in the garage?"

The vic? What was this, some kind of crime serial on TV? "That's right. I went in there to get a look at the hearse. I thought maybe I could sell it and use the money to keep making repairs to this place. Do you know anyone who wants a vintage hearse?"

Archer pulled a face that clearly said he didn't know anyone with that kind of taste in cars.

"Did the guy break into the funeral home?" Archer asked.

"Not that I'm aware of. I don't even know if he was killed here on the property. The chief constable says the garage might just have been the killer's hiding place."

"Why would the vic or the killer be here in the first place, though?" Archer mused. "This place has been abandoned for so long. Why come here at all?"

"Believe me, I've been asking myself the same questions. If you get any of those answers, you let me know, okay?"

"Yeah. Anyway, I'm heading up to the attic. It's time to find out just how bad the wiring up there is."

"Good luck." Working on the wainscoting had been a good way to push the murder out of my thoughts for a while. Archer's questions had brought it all crashing back. My one consolation was that I felt a little safer knowing someone was in the house with me, even if Archer was all the way up in the attic.

Jo called just as I was finishing up a sandwich to say she had time to come by later with her stuff. "Can I stay there tonight? I'm anxious to get settled into my new digs!"

"Of course," I said immediately. A good night's sleep suddenly looked like a real possibility, since I knew I would be more comfortable if I wasn't alone in the house.

So, two hours later, Jo pulled up in front of the house in a small moving truck. She had clearly been packed up already when she called to ask if she could move in that day. I told her to pull around to the back, where a ramp led up into the back of the house. It had been the way bodies came and went from the funeral home.

I met Jo at the ramp with a slightly rusted gurney that I had found in the embalming room. There had been a lot of other equipment, too, and the first thing I had done after moving in was call the nearest junkyard to haul it all away. The stainless steel gurney, however, I had kept. It made a nice cart for shuttling things, like moving boxes.

Jo laughed heartily at the sight of me wheeling the gurney toward the back of the moving truck. "Practical" was her only comment.

We quickly loaded the gurney with boxes, then wheeled everything inside to drop it all in the bedroom Jo had chosen. When we emerged into the backyard to make a second run, I spotted a large white bird landing on top of the moving truck. Its wingspan was at least six feet, and its saggy yellow beak made me think of someone with a double chin.

"Hazel, meet Gordon." Jo smiled proudly at the pelican. "I know it's an unusual familiar, but he's really great."

I called a hello to the bird, who let out a craggy squawk in response.

There was a flash of brown in my peripheral vision, and I saw Perkins flying past me. He seemed undaunted by Gordon's size, because he flew right up to the pelican, fluttering to a rest next to him. Perkins only came up to Gordon's round midsection, and Gordon extended a wing, curling it gently behind the burrowing owl.

Jo giggled. "Aren't they cute together?"

"Very cute," I agreed.

We were unloading more boxes into Jo's bedroom when she said, "I just finished a story about the murder for tomorrow's edition of the newspaper."

"Tomorrow? But, my electrician said he read about it in today's paper."

"That was just a short piece. Tomorrow's story has a lot more detail. I almost called you for a quote, but I figured you never met Steve, anyway."

"You're right. Who's Steve?"

"Oh, didn't the constables tell you? Steve Zillmann is the murder victim. He owned a delivery truck, and he hauled stuff for half the businesses in this town."

EIGHT

"A DELIVERY TRUCK?" I repeated. When Jo nodded, I told her about my job conversation with Valerian. "This explains why the bar hasn't been getting their beer and liquor deliveries. Valerian said the driver was nowhere to be found."

"Until you did, in fact, find him." Jo frowned. "I should have called you for a quote, after all. You could have given me the exclusive about the moment of discovery."

I shook my head. "It wouldn't have been much of a quote. I pulled a tarp off the back of the hearse, and I realized the pile of fabric underneath the bumper had an arm in it."

Jo gasped. "The killer chopped off Steve's arm? The police didn't tell me that!"

I wrinkled my nose at that mental image. "No, he was all in one piece. His arm was all I could see, I meant."

"Good. I would hate to have to run back to the office to amend the story. Though, I have to say, there's some part of me that has always wanted to dash in at the last minute and shout, 'Stop the presses!' Just for the drama of it, you know?"

"Did the police share any other juicy details with you?"

"No. Chief Constable Hightower was pretty tight-lipped, but it's clear the constables don't know why someone killed Steve, or why he was stashed in your garage. Hightower did imply Steve wasn't actually killed inside the garage, but that doesn't mean much. It could have happened in your backyard or miles away."

I shuddered at the idea of Steve meeting his end just feet from where I slept every night. "You said you're really good at manifesting things if you write them down. Can you write an intention about how this murder is already solved, and the entire investigation went really smoothly?"

"It's probably best if I don't." Jo plunked a box labeled *Photos* onto the rug. "There's a reason I write for the newspaper instead of having a business that helps people manifest their dreams."

"I do recall you writing you wanted your new room to be a laid-back space." I tapped the toe of my sneaker against the floor. "You were thinking about relaxation, not a sloped floor."

"That's far from the worst, though. When I was fifteen, I had a huge crush on a guy. I wrote that I wanted him to notice me, and that I wanted him to be so enthralled by me that he wouldn't even look at anyone else. The next day, we were in art class, and someone dumped half a can of blue paint down the front of my shirt. The whole class laughed at me, including the guy. He noticed me, all right, and he stared at me, laughing, for the rest of the period."

"Oh, Jo, that's terrible. What a horrible thing for any-one to experience, let alone a teenager. We're all so self-conscious at that age."

"It was a valuable lesson, though. I already knew I was a good writer, and that incident taught me to focus on writing about the past rather than the future. I can't screw up something if it already happened. Maybe I'm not so good at shaping my future, but I'm a great re-porter."

Knowing about Jo's misadventures with magic made me like her even more. Growing up, I had always felt intimidated by witches who were either extremely pow-erful or always perfect. Or, worse, both. Talk about something to make a teenager self-conscious. My magic had always been decent, but never great. Leaving Fox-fire Haven and heading to the mundane world had felt freeing because I was no longer comparing myself to powerful witches.

Once we had Jo's boxes and some smaller furniture inside the room, we had to enlist Archer's help to bring in the bed. He seemed happy for an excuse to get out of the attic, and I had to point out that he had a cobweb tangled in his hair.

Eventually, though, the moving truck was empty. Even Gordon and Perkins had flown off, and I hoped the two of them were enjoying getting to know each other. Gordon was so big I had zero worry about Wyatt's cat coming after Perkins. Yes, Jo's familiar was an unusual one, but he was going to be a great bodyguard for my owl.

"How about I make us dinner?" I asked Jo as she began to dig into the nearest box. Archer had left, saying he would be back to keep working on the attic wiring the next morning, and the sun was just about to dip below the hills on the horizon. "You can get some unpacking done while I cook."

"I would appreciate it! I'm not a great chef myself, though my ex did love a salmon dish that I used to make him. Holler when it's time to eat."

As I got a pot of water boiling so I could cook pasta, I realized I felt good. I had been looking forward to Jo's arrival simply so I wouldn't be alone in the house while a killer was on the loose, but as it turned out, I was enjoying having the company.

Maybe this roommate thing is going to work out well, after all.

That thought was quickly followed by another, which was that having one roommate who had just moved in a couple hours before was very different from having three renters who were there every day, week after week and month after month.

One person and one day at a time, Haze.

Once dinner was ready, I went down the hallway to find Jo arranging framed photos on her nightstand. She had done an impressive amount of unpacking in the short time it had taken for me to make dinner, and she was eager for the break.

I had set the table in the dining room, and I had even opened a bottle of wine. We toasted to Jo's arrival, then dug into our food. Once we were done, she seemed reluctant to go back to unpacking, suggesting we refill our wine glasses and sit on the front porch, instead. I readily agreed, and soon, we were both settled into the wicker chairs on the porch, looking out at low clouds speeding across the starry sky.

"Chief Constable Hightower doesn't seem to be a big fan of yours," Jo remarked. "To hear him tell the tale, you just about put handcuffs on him for allowing his cat to get near Perkins."

I had just taken a sip of wine, and I choked it down as I started to laugh. "I wasn't that mean to him. He's the one who acted like a jerk."

"I saw his car outside the tavern on my way over here today. I guess you've driven him to day drinking, since that was at four o'clock this afternoon."

"It's more likely he was there trying to trace Steve's last steps. Or last deliveries, I should say. Wyatt and I aren't going to be friendly neighbors anytime soon, but I don't think I'm so awful that he had to go drown his sorrows at the tavern."

"I wonder who the last person to see Steve alive was. Other than the killer, of course. I guess that's what the constables are trying to figure out."

"That, and how long he was stashed in my garage before I found him. If Wyatt thinks I'm a suspect, though, then that must mean the constables believe Steve was killed sometime after I moved back to town."

"The chief did mention they thought Steve had been there for about two weeks."

"Oh! Valerian said he stopped showing up for delivery runs about then."

Had I been home when Steve's body was shoved underneath the hearse?

We continued to sip our wine in silence for a while. It was a chilly evening, and I was glad I had pulled on a thick cardigan before stepping onto the front porch. Still, after being cooped up inside the house for so much of the day, the fresh air felt good against my face. As we watched, Gordon and Perkins swooped into view, landing on the porch railing next to each other.

"I think Gordon is going to like it here," Jo said. I looked over to see a contented smile on her face. "And so am I."

As I'd hoped, I slept like the dead that night. After such a pleasant evening, I went to bed thinking about cute familiars and good company rather than Steve Zillmann.

Jo was up and out of the house by seven o'clock the next morning, saying she was going to return the moving truck before heading to the newspaper office. I had been only half-awake, the coffee still brewing and my eyes still trying to focus, as she breezed out of the kitchen, telling me to have a good day in a singsong voice.

I had found the flaw in having Jo as a renter. She was a morning person.

By midmorning, I headed out, too. There were several errands around town that I needed to take care of, and since one of those was picking up groceries, I drove into downtown rather than walking. The constable station was between me and the supermarket, and on a whim, I drove into the parking lot in front of the station. Wyatt hadn't bothered to tell me the murder victim in my garage had been identified, but if I paid him a visit, maybe he would give me some more details.

Except, when I went inside the station, the man at the front desk informed me Wyatt was out. "Can you please ask him to call me?" I asked. "I'm Hazel Underwood."

"Ah, you're the one who found the strangle victim. Sure, I'll tell him to give you a buzz later."

Steve was strangled. I had gotten some more information about the murder, and I hadn't even had to talk to Wyatt. It was a win-win for me.

My next stop was the tavern, which had just opened up for customers who wanted an early lunch. Valerian still hadn't told me when she would be moving in, so I wanted to make plans with her.

Plus, I wanted to know why Wyatt had been there the previous afternoon.

The first thing I saw when I walked into the tavern was the Bigfoot, who was perched on the same stool he had occupied during my previous visit. He was hunched over a glass of whiskey again, and Valerian was standing at the opposite end of the bar, giving him plenty of space.

I hopped up onto the stool closest to Valerian. "Everything okay?" I asked, flicking my eyes in Barry's direction.

"He started early today, but he's not giving me any trouble, if that's what you mean."

"Good. I thought I'd drop by so we can pick your move-in date."

Valerian propped her elbows on the bar. "I won't be moving in if I'm in jail."

I tilted my head and peered at Valerian, trying to figure out if she was making a joke. There wasn't a trace of humor in her expression. "Why would you be in jail?"

"Because the chief constable stopped in here yesterday to ask me if I'm the one who killed Steve Zillmann."

NINE

"WHY WOULD YOU BE accused of murdering the delivery guy?" I asked.

Valerian put a hand against her chest. "I'm a no-nonsense lady. Steve, on the other hand, was an irresponsible, disrespectful jerk. The guy was in his thirties, but most days, he acted like a surly preteen. One day, he came in two hours late to pick up beer crates that needed to go back to the distributor, looking like he'd just dragged himself out of bed. I called him out on being unprofessional, and he started yelling. I yelled right back and said I wouldn't allow anyone to treat me that way in my own bar. He said it wasn't my bar. I was just the hired help. Then—oh, it doesn't matter. The point is, Steve and I had a big fight, right there in front of everyone."

"Which means Wyatt put you on his suspect list. I wonder if your name is above or below mine?"

Valerian barked out a laugh. "You can't be serious. Why would he suspect you?"

"Because I don't like his cat."

"More proof that Wyatt is grasping at straws. My fight with Steve was three years ago. Steve and I never apologized to each other, but he started arriving closer to his scheduled times, and while we were never going to be best buddies, we made it work. I'm about as likely to have murdered Steve as you."

"If you were the one who murdered Steve, then it would be remarkable that you stashed his body at the funeral home, then rented out a room at the very same place. Maybe Wyatt thinks you're psychic, and he suspects you saw your future home there and decided to hide Steve's body where you could keep a close eye on it."

"I wish I could see the future! I could have saved myself from a lot of past mistakes." Valerian's gaze fixed on a spot somewhere behind me, and I wondered what memories she was recalling. Suddenly, she gave herself a shake. "No, my thing is potions. But instead of having a high-paying job in pharmaceuticals or chemistry, I mix a different kind of potion." To illustrate her point, Valerian raised an empty pint glass.

"And I'm sure your potion-making skills are very much appreciated by the tavern patrons."

"It's not a bad job. I like hearing people's stories, and my regulars are a pretty good crew. Even Roscoe is tolerable, sometimes. Plus, being a bartender is a whole lot better than my cousin's job. He's a potion witch who specializes in fertilizer. That stuff takes magic and a whole lot of cow—well, you know. So smelly."

I'd never stopped to think about fertilizer being made with magic, but it would explain why I'd never seen flowers as big and bright as the ones I'd grown up admiring around Foxfire Haven.

"You just mentioned Roscoe," I said. "Surely, there are some other not-so-nice people who come to the tavern. Maybe one of them killed Steve."

Valerian looked around the mostly empty tavern, probably picturing the regulars who frequented the place. "I suppose it's possible, though I think it's unlikely. Roscoe is mean to everyone, but I don't think he'd kill anyone. For one thing, it would just take too much effort. Why murder someone, when you could be here having a pint, instead?"

"Who else did Steve make deliveries for? Maybe someone else he worked with is the killer."

"He worked for a lot of the small businesses in town. The hobby shop, the gift and stationery shop—if you haven't been to Stacy's yet, you should go check out her magical teacups. They keep your tea warm for hours! Um, let's see. Steve made plant deliveries for the garden store. He did stuff for the magic store..."

I laughed softly. "Basically, Steve worked with all of downtown."

"Pretty much. The constables are going to have a lot of folks to talk to."

"Good. If the chief constable is busy, then he won't have time to harass me."

"Speaking of time, how about I move in on Saturday? I can easily finish my packing by then, and it gives me a few days to sort out how I'm getting it all over to the funeral home."

"Sounds good to me."

I said goodbye to Valerian, then finally made my way to the supermarket. I was so busy thinking about what she'd told me about Steve and the many people in Foxfire Haven he'd done business with that I barely paid attention to what I was putting in my shopping cart. I was surprised, then, when I got home and discovered I'd bought two types of bread but no cheese and lunchmeat to make sandwiches with it.

At least I had a jar of peanut butter at home, so lunch wasn't a loss.

After lunch, I put the first layer of fresh white paint on the wainscoting in the dining room, my mind still on the murder as I painted. I told myself the constables were working on leads, but sitting at home doing nothing about the murder was making me restless.

Someone had been murdered, and their body had been stashed in my garage. I was taking it personally.

I decided it wouldn't hurt to do some asking around myself, so I secured the lid on the paint and put on fresh clothes that weren't spattered with tiny white specks, then headed back into town. Instead of walking or driving, I rode a squeaky, rusted old bicycle I had found on the back porch. There was a wire basket on the front and a bell that gave a slow, wheezing ring when I sounded it. I'd had to pump up the tires when I found the bike, but so far, it was holding up for me.

Valerian had mentioned the hobby shop, and I remembered exactly where it was from passing it every day to and from school. There was a railroad crossing sign hanging next to the door, so it was impossible to miss. I decided to start my little murder investigation there.

The owner of the hobby shop was a rail-thin man who looked like he was at least eighty years old. When I introduced myself and said I was just asking around to learn more about Steve, the man squinted at me through thick glasses. "I'd heard the funeral home was open again."

"Not open for business, but open for renters to live there."

"Live there? Ah, I'm not interested. I've got one foot in the grave already, and moving to a funeral home seems like too much of an invitation for the Grim Reaper to come collect me."

It took some time to get the man onto the subject of Steve, but I didn't learn anything useful. The man said Steve's hair was too long for his taste, but his rate was good, and he was always nice enough to place the boxes he'd delivered onto the shelves in the storage room.

My next stop was Stacy's Stationery and Sundries. I resisted the urge to browse the magical self-warming teacups Valerian had mentioned. One might be a nice treat once I had paid for some of the repairs to the funeral home, but at the moment, I was just there to get some information.

I found Stacy herself behind a giant stack of pastel envelopes. Her blouse was the same shade of lilac as the stationery she was writing on. She greeted me warmly, saying she had seen one of my flyers for the available rooms just that morning. "Someone was in here recently saying they were looking for a place to live," Stacy added. "But, for the life of me, I can't remember who it was."

"Hopefully that person sees the flyer, too. I still have one room open."

Stacy clicked her tongue. "It's a shame about Steve Zillmann, isn't it? You must have been horrified when you found him!"

"It was a shock, yes. In fact, he's the reason I came in here. I'm trying to learn more about him, because I didn't know him at all, and I just can't understand why anyone would kill him."

"I can't understand it, either. He was never on time with deliveries, but he was a decent guy. He always had a smile for me, and it's hard to believe I'll never see it again." Stacy gestured toward a mostly empty shelf. "I need to restock, but I have to be here to mind the store. I need someone to run to the warehouse to grab things for me."

"Good luck finding someone new," I said. In a big city, it would be an easy task. In a town as small as Foxfire Haven, it was probably going to be a challenge.

I was beginning to have sympathy for Wyatt, imagining him talking to the same people and not getting any insight into who might have murdered Steve, or why.

Then, I remembered his attitude toward both Perkins and me, and all that sympathy shot right out the window.

Third time is the charm, I told myself as I headed for the garden store. Even if I didn't get any juicy details about Steve, I decided I was going to splurge and buy a few flowers. I would only get enough to fit into the basket on the front of the bicycle, so I couldn't be tempted to overspend.

Petunia was with a customer in the fruit tree aisle when I arrived, so I pretended to be browsing miniature apple trees while I waited. Once she was free, I gave her a wave. "Good to see you again," I said.

"How is your search for renters going?" Petunia smiled. "You renting out rooms in the old funeral home is quite the gossip today."

"I've filled two of the three rooms. If you hear of anyone looking for a place, please let them know I have a beautiful room with stained-glass windows available."

Petunia pressed a finger to her lips. "Someone recently said they were looking for a place. Who was it? So many people are in here every day that I can't remember. But if I do think of it, I'll let you know. Now, what can I help you with?"

"If everyone is gossiping about me turning the funeral home into a home for living people, then I'm sure they're also gossiping about Steve's murder."

Petunia's face looked strained, and I recognized it as the expression people make just before tears come.

"I'm so sorry," I said. "That was a rude thing for me to say. My condolences if he was a friend of yours."

"He wasn't a friend, but I knew him for a long time. Steve probably saw more backyards around this town than anyone else, since he delivered so many plants to my customers." Petunia's face relaxed, and I stopped worrying she was about to cry. Instead, she sounded frustrated as she continued talking. "What am I going to do? Who will deliver plants to people who don't have cars big enough for their orders? How am I going to get flower arrangements to weddings?"

"You're a florist, too?" I asked.

"Of course. No one grows flowers as well as I do."

I had to wonder if Petunia used that stinky, magical fertilizer that Valerian's cousin worked on.

"Stacy over at the stationery shop is in the same boat," I said. "I hope you find a new delivery person soon."

Petunia nodded thoughtfully. "Yeah. My uncle has a pickup truck. Maybe I could borrow it from him. My sister is an interior designer, and she has a little trailer. Hmm."

I said goodbye to Petunia, but I wasn't sure if she had even heard me. She was busy making a list of people who might be able to help her out of her delivery dilemma.

The garden store had been another dead end for learning anything useful about Steve, but I headed to a display of small daisies while trying to figure out how many flower containers would fit in the bicycle's basket.

I was balancing three plants when the gnome sidled up to me. "You're trying to help the constables, aren't you?" he asked in an undertone, not even looking at me.

"I'm trying to help myself," I admitted. "I want to know why someone killed Steve Zillmann, then left his body in my garage."

The gnome—Gnorris, I remembered Petunia having called him—reached out to straighten a row of flowers. He was quiet for a moment before saying, "I don't know why they picked your garage, but I can tell you who did it."

Ten

GNORRIS WAS STILL REFUSING to look at me, so I decided to play his game. I kept my eyes fixed on the flowers in front of me, pretending I was still browsing. Casually, as if I were asking about the recommended amount of sunshine for the plants I was carrying, I asked, "Have you told the police that you know who killed Steve?"

"Well. No. I, um..." Gnorris broke off and cleared his throat. I glanced down and saw him nervously stroking his long white beard. "I don't know for certain, but I have a hunch."

"In that case, have you told the police your hunch?"

Finally, that got Gnorris to look up at me. "No! If I told the police, and she found out, she might curse me before they can lock her away. She's not a witch, but she can work some magic when she wants to."

"Gnorris, are you going to tell me who this person is, or not?" I was quickly losing my patience, but I added, in what I hoped was an encouraging tone, "I won't tell anyone where I got the tip."

At least a minute stretched by as Gnorris sighed, huffed, and even stomped over to a lavender bush. Finally, he moved so close to me his shoulder brushed my knee. "Adeline Beaumont. The owner of Into the Cauldron."

When I gave Gnorris a confused look, he added, "The magical supply store. Steve was making late-night deliveries to her, out in the alley behind the store. And I mean middle-of-the-night late. I knew the first time I saw it that the two of them were up to something."

"If being out in the middle of the night is enough reason to suspect someone of murder, then what were you doing out at that hour?"

"Walking home from the tavern, of course."

"How many times did you see the deliveries happening?"

"A few times. I first saw it a couple months before Steve disappeared. Of course, I figured he'd just skipped town, or maybe went on vacation without remembering to tell anyone. I never thought someone would kill him."

"Did you know Steve well?"

"No," Gnorris answered quickly.

I wasn't sure I believed that answer. Still, Gnorris had given me the first bit of useful information about Steve, and I wasn't going to push. It sounded like this Adeline Beaumont was someone to look into, so I would have to go to the magical supply store to follow up.

Except, I really, really didn't want to do that. It wasn't that I was afraid of standing face-to-face with a possible killer. No, it was the idea of walking into a shop selling nothing but magical supplies that made a shudder run from the tips of my toes to the top of my head.

I still hadn't used my magic since returning to Foxfire Haven. It had been years since I had been a practicing witch, and if I waltzed into a magic store, it might trigger an event.

Wyatt's accusatory stare as he'd told me about his conversation with my daughter, Tara, came back to me. That look that said he thought I was trouble, and possibly even dangerous.

I thanked Gnorris for sharing the information about Adeline with me, then bought my flowers and loaded them into the basket on my bicycle. As I pedaled away, the wheels squeaking loudly, I tried to build up the courage to head straight for Into the Cauldron. I had to pass it on the way home, so there was no reason not to stop.

Other than fear, of course.

My cell phone began to ring shortly before I reached the store, so I pulled to a stop at the side of the road and dug it out of my purse. I was hoping it was someone calling about the third available room, but instead, I heard Wyatt's voice on the other end.

"We're done going over the hearse," he said gruffly, not even bothering to identify himself first. "Come and get it as soon as you can, because that giant thing is taking up half the garage."

"I'll be right there," I promised.

"Oh, and I changed the oil in it. And the brake pads. Air filter, too. The thing was a death trap. But you'll need to take care of the insurance and registration before you can drive it anywhere but straight home."

As Wyatt had been talking, my brow had furrowed deeper with every word. He had done work on the hearse? Why would he do something so nice for me?

He'll probably present me with a bill as soon as I step foot inside the constable station.

Still, a hearse that was running better would get me more money. "Thank you very much," I said, slightly surprised to hear the sincerity in my tone. "I'm just a few blocks away, so I'll come get it now, and I'll go right home, like you said."

"Good. I'd hate to hear you got a ticket from one of our constables for driving an uninsured vehicle. We'd much rather be spending our time solving the murder instead of pulling you over."

"How is the investigation going? Do you have any updates for me?"

"There's nothing I can share at this time. Just be grateful we haven't hauled you in for further questioning."

I wanted to retort, but I wisely kept my mouth shut. Wyatt really knew how to push my buttons, and I wondered if he delighted in it. I had thanked him for working on the hearse, but I certainly wan't going to thank him for not arresting me, when there was zero reason to think I had murdered Steve.

"Have a nice day, Chief Constable," I said, ending the call before Wyatt could respond.

I put away my phone and began pedaling again, now heading for the constable station rather than the magic store. I wasn't sure which of the two I felt the most dread about.

When I went inside the station, the same man who had been sitting at the desk previously was there again. He barely glanced at me before he jerked a thumb over his shoulder. "It's around back, in the garage. The keys are in it."

Sure enough, the hearse was sitting just inside one of three wide roll-up metal doors at the back of the station. A couple of the sedans the force used for patrolling were in the garage, too, and a mechanic waved a wrench in greeting when I walked in.

I had never driven a vehicle as giant as a hearse, and I took my sweet time backing it out of the warehouse. The engine rumbled moodily.

In fact, it kind of sounded like Wyatt.

Once I was out of the warehouse and moving forward, I felt a little more confident. I had driven rental vans over the years, taking Tara and her friends camping or off to a little town for a weekend. The hearse was bigger than any of those vans, but it felt manageable. I wouldn't have wanted to drive the crowded, steep streets of San Francisco in it, but tooling around Foxfire Haven would be okay.

My bicycle was parked in front of the station, so I stopped and loaded it into the back of the hearse. I nestled the flowers on the floor of the passenger seat, so they wouldn't tip over and spill dirt all over the place.

As I pulled out of the parking lot, I pumped my fist. "Yes! Hearse acquired, and not a single cranky old man in sight!"

And, I noticed, someone—possibly Wyatt—had filled up the gas tank.

I had promised to head straight home after picking up the hearse, but I did make one detour. There was a sign on the road that read *Auto Wash*, with an arrow pointing to the right. I turned down the side street and easily found the little self-serve car wash. The hearse wasn't that dirty, since it had been stored underneath the tarps, but I didn't like the idea of driving around a vehicle that had been the hiding place for a dead body. Even though Steve had been under the hearse instead of inside it, I still wanted to wash off any dead-guy residue that might be lingering on the rear bumper.

It wasn't until I was pulling into my driveway that I realized I should have asked Wyatt if I was allowed to use my garage again. I didn't want to call and ask at the moment, so I pulled up right in front of the house on the circular drive rather than heading down the narrower lane that led to the garage in the backyard.

I took a step back to appreciate just how dramatic the hearse and old funeral home looked together. The black hearse looked picture-perfect against the white columns on the front porch and the stained-glass windows of the chapel rooms. The funeral home's red brick exterior could stand a good pressure-washing, but the place was still elegant-looking, even after so many decades of service.

Then, I noticed that one of the dormer windows in the attic space had a broken pane. Another item that would have to be fixed.

I eyed the hearse. "Time for a glow-up," I said. As soon as I got the interior cleaned, I could take photos and make a sales post online. Maybe I would print up some flyers and drive them to the nearest mundane towns, too. Someone in the region had to want a hearse, and I was determined to find them.

The weather was cloudy and cool, perfect for doing work in the driveway. I unloaded the flowers and my bicycle, then grabbed rags, window cleaner, and the same upholstery cleaner I'd been using on the dining room rug.

An hour later, the inside of the hearse still looked shabby, but at least it was gleaming. Before I could bask in the glow of a job well done, though, I realized I had forgotten to clean out the glovebox. Maybe I'd find the hearse's most recent registration card inside, so I would know what year and model it was.

The registration card was on top of a small pile of things inside the glovebox, and it informed me that I was in possession of a 1978 Cadillac Hearse Wagon. Under the card was a folded map of Foxfire Haven, a small case containing Uncle Grant's business cards, and a stack of greeting cards and photographs.

I had no idea why the cards and photos were in the glovebox, unless Grant had simply enjoyed having some keepsakes along for the ride with him. He had probably spent a fair amount of time sitting outside churches, waiting for funerals to conclude, and I could imagine him flipping through greetings from friends and family members while waiting to take a coffin to the cemetery.

There was even a photo of my brother and me in the collection. I looked like I was about seven years old, and my brother and I had rummaged through our parents' clothes to make ourselves look like pirates. I was brandishing a sword made from a skinny tree branch, and my mother's red scarf was tied around my waist like a sash.

I was enjoying the faded old photos, especially since I recognized so many family members in them. One photo was of Grant, who looked like he was in his twenties when it had been taken. He had one arm slung around another man's shoulders, and they were both holding up medals dangling from blue ribbons.

The man Grant was with looked familiar, but I couldn't place him, at first. I mentally listed off my uncles, aunts, and cousins, but none of them looked like this man. Why, then, did I know his face?

It suddenly hit me as I imagined that face with a wrinkled forehead and a disdainful frown. I pictured the face in full size, just inches from mine.

At some point in time, my Uncle Grant had been good friends with the very man who, just days before, had bad-talked my family and told me how weird Grant was. The man in the photo was Roscoe Palladano.

ELeven

I STARED AT THE photo of Grant and Roscoe for a long time, my brain trying to process the fact that the two of them had once been friends. I wondered what kind of event could have made Roscoe so hateful about Grant now, and I thought about Roscoe's claim that Grant had gotten, as he called it, "weird." What had happened?

And, I wondered, was Roscoe behind Steve's murder? Maybe he had purposely planted Steve at the funeral home to discredit my family.

I shook my head. That was an outlandish theory. Grant had died six years before, so it seemed a little late for Roscoe to try to tarnish his name.

Unless Roscoe was trying to make me look bad, instead.

With a huff, I threw the photo onto the passenger seat of the hearse. I wouldn't know anything for certain until I talked to Roscoe, but I wanted to do that even less than I wanted to talk to the owner of Into the Cauldron.

I grabbed everything that had been inside the glovebox and went into the house, stashing the items in an empty drawer in the kitchen. I could sort through all of it later and decide what was worth keeping. At the moment, I wanted a snack. I had worked up an appetite with the cleaning, but it wasn't quite dinnertime yet.

I grabbed a bag of tortilla chips and a jar of salsa, then plopped down at the table in the breakfast nook of the kitchen.

Perkins had been asleep in his little nest by the heater, but he flitted over to me and perched on the back of one of the chairs as I scarfed down the chips.

"Oh, lady, what are you doing?" I heard Holman say from behind me.

I turned toward him. "Eating," I said around a mouthful of chips and salsa.

"Don't come crying to me when your dungarees no longer fit."

"They're called jeans, and I'll be just fine, thank you very much. Remember that talk we had the other day about being nice to my prospective renters? You should try being more polite to me, too."

Holman drifted forward so he was next to me at the table. His body lowered, as if he were sitting in the chair Perkins was perched on. As a ghost, he couldn't really sit down, so I wasn't quite sure how that worked for him. "I am being polite. You're a nice-looking gal, Hazel. I'm trying to help you stay that way."

I raised a finger. "Body-shaming is not polite. Were you this forthright with people when you were living?"

"Certainly not. I had to hold my tongue all the time. But, now that I'm a ghost, I can say whatever I want, and no one can punch me in the face for it."

"Just because you can say something without facing consequences for it, doesn't mean you should." My finger was still in the air, and I felt like I was lecturing a wayward child. I had already raised Tara. Was I going to have to raise a ghost, too?

I turned toward the doorway when I heard approaching footsteps. It was Jo, who strode into the kitchen with a white plastic bag in one hand. "Hi! I got takeout. I hope you like Chinese?"

"I do, but I'm sure Holman will warn us about the danger noodles present to our dainty little—" I turned slightly as I gestured toward the ghost, but he had disappeared. "Never mind. Thank you for picking up food."

Soon, Jo and I were seated at the dining room table, digging into our dinner. "I know it's kind of early to eat," Jo said between bites, "but I never got a lunch break today."

I waved my fork in the air. "No complaints here. After my day, I might even get some ice cream out of the freezer once we finish dinner." I went on to fill Jo in on my search for information about Steve, and Gnorris's hints that the killer might be Adeline Beaumont, the owner of Into the Cauldron.

Of all the reactions I had expected from Jo, laughter was not one of them. "Of course Steve was making late-night deliveries to the magic store!" Jo said once her mirth had died down. "Adeline is a vampire. Everyone in town knows that. She's got staff to run the store during the day, and she comes in after dark. It's actually really convenient, because I know I can stop by and stock up on magical supplies after a late night at work."

I slowly poked at a piece of chicken with my fork. "Then was Gnorris trying to frame her by implying she and Steve were up to something? Or, perhaps, nighttime deliveries are normal, but two o'clock in the morning ones aren't."

"You should definitely talk to Adeline." Jo leaned forward, an excited expression on her face. "What if Gnorris is the killer, and he's trying to deflect attention away from himself? Oh, I can see the headline now: *Vampire Framed for Gnome's Killing Spree.*"

"One murder doesn't constitute a spree," I pointed out.

"True. The headline will need work, but I'm going to make sure I'm the one who gets to write the story. Hazel, you have to keep me apprised of every little detail, so I have the inside scoop. I'll have the first draft of the story written before they're even done fingerprinting Gnorris at the constable station!"

The mental image of an eighteen-inch-high gnome getting his fingerprints taken was funny to me, but it also made me think of one flaw in Jo's theory. "Even if he was the killer, then how in the world did Gnorris drag Steve's body under the hearse? He's not strong enough to do something like that."

"Maybe he had an accomplice," Jo speculated. "Or, maybe, he's not the killer at all."

She looked disappointed that we hadn't solved the murder while having a casual chat over dinner, so I consoled her with, "I promise to talk to Adeline tomorrow night, and I'll tell you everything I learn."

Knowing Adeline was a vampire made me feel an excited anticipation that almost overshadowed my fear of being inside a magic store. I had only ever seen vampires in passing while growing up in Foxfire Haven, and even though I knew they were just like any other member of society—with the exception of being undead, of course—I was rather looking forward to meeting one face-to-face.

The next morning, my first order of business was getting the insurance and registration squared away for the hearse. There had been some rain overnight, but the morning was looking like it would stay dry, so I very optimistically rode my bicycle to the DMV.

Things were predictably slow there, and I found myself wishing there was a magic spell to speed things up. By the time I had the paperwork for the hearse sorted out and a new license plate for it, my stomach was rumbling.

There was a cafe I had passed on my trips downtown, so I decided to treat myself to lunch there rather than heading home right away. The Salt Circle Cafe had a neon sign out front depicting a white circle surrounding a plate of bacon and eggs.

Anyone passing through who was unaware that Foxfire Haven was a magical town would probably think it was a strange name. Considering I had a snarky ghost haunting my home, I appreciated the nod to the spiritually protective power of salt. A circle of salt created an impenetrable barrier for ghosts, keeping anyone inside the circle safe from malicious spirits.

I also had to laugh at the cafe's tagline: *Protecting your taste buds since 1947!*

The cafe's menu said breakfast was available all day, but I opted for a chef salad, instead. As I waited for my salad, I let my eyes wander around the long, narrow space. There were booths on either side, and the servers were adept at dancing around each other as they bustled to and from the kitchen.

The walls were decorated with photographs of famous people who had visited the cafe. Famous, at least, in the magical world. There were no movie stars or pop singers on the walls, with the exception of a woman who had a slew of folk hits in the nineteen sixties. She had been a witch, though she claimed she hadn't used any magic to get her songs to the top of the charts.

When my salad arrived, my server gave me a long look. "You're new in town," she said. It wasn't a question.

"Yes. I just moved into the old funeral home."

"Oh, you're the one looking for renters, right? I saw the flyer. I was just having a chat with someone who said she was looking for a new place to live, but I can't remember who it was. Oh, let me think. This would have been a couple days ago. Well, don't let me stop you from eating. If I remember, I'll let you know."

I'd had to stifle a chuckle as the server spoke. She was the third person who had claimed someone in town was looking for a room to rent but couldn't remember who that person was. Either there were several potential renters, or there was one person who was woefully forgettable.

After lunch, I was heading for my bicycle, when I spotted a woman across the street who was clearly having a rough day. She had a stack of at least fifteen white folding chairs behind her, and she was trying to load them into the back of her compact SUV.

There was absolutely no way all of those chairs were going to fit. As I watched, she got one of the chairs wedged on top of the ones already inside the SUV, then stopped and wiped a hand across her brow. Her straight dark hair was in a ponytail, but strands had slipped out and stuck to her face and neck.

The woman was a stranger to me, but I felt so bad for her that I found myself dashing across the street to offer help before I even realized what I was doing. "Hey, do you need a hand?" I called.

The woman looked at me, defeat in her brown eyes. "What I need is Steve and his truck. I've got a wedding this weekend, and I don't know how I'm going to get everything set up in time without him to help me."

Steve really had been the go-to delivery person for Foxfire Haven.

"You're getting married this weekend?" I asked, preparing to give my congratulations.

"No. I'm a wedding and event planner. My client is having an evening ceremony in the park tomorrow night." The woman wiped her hand on her pink-and-purple floral dress, then extended it to me. "Marlee Yamada. I own Enchanted Events."

"I'm Hazel Underwood, and I have something even better than a truck. If you give me about twenty minutes, I'll be able to help you load these chairs up."

Marlee nodded her head in the direction of the cafe. "Sounds like just enough time for me to get an iced tea. See you soon, and thank you."

If I had surprised myself by offering to help Marlee in the first place, I was even more surprised by this out-of-my-way plan that had popped into my head. As I pedaled home, I wondered why I was so eager to help out.

Maybe, I realized, *because it's the kind of help I wanted when I moved here.*

But I had been too stubborn to ask for it, and too embarrassed to tell people why I was back in Foxfire Haven.

When I got home, I quickly screwed the temporary license plate I'd gotten at the DMV onto the rear bumper of the hearse, then drove back to town. I realized by the time I reached downtown that I was smiling. I was helping someone out, and it felt good.

Marlee was waiting for me, sitting on a bench near her car and the stack of chairs. I saw her glance at the hearse with casual curiosity, but her face broke into a surprised grin when she saw me behind the wheel. The hulking vehicle was far too big for me to flip a U-turn in the street, so I cruised right past Marlee and turned around in a parking lot.

By the time I pulled up to the curb behind Marlee's car, she was on her feet, her hands clasped in front of her.

"This is absolutely brilliant!" Marlee squealed as I climbed out of the hearse. "And I recruited some help, so you and I don't have to load all the chairs ourselves."

A man was standing a short distance away, talking on a cell phone. When Marlee pointed at him, he gave us both a wave.

"That's the groom," she said. "He walked past while I was waiting for you, and he offered to help. I hope he doesn't think I'm going to give the bride's family a discount, just because he's pitching in."

"I'm sure he's only doing it to be nice," I said.

The man ended his call, said hello to me, and then the three of us got to work loading the chairs into the hearse. It was done in just minutes.

Since the wedding was being held at the park in front of the town hall, that meant I only had to drive four blocks to reach our destination. We unloaded the chairs as quickly as we had put them in, and before long, I was standing with Marlee in the shade of a towering magnolia tree in the middle of the park.

Marlee had a small purse slung across her body, and she unzipped it. "I don't have a lot of cash on me, but I need to give you something."

"Oh, no, that's not necessary," I said quickly. "I just wanted to be helpful."

"Then how about this: if you come back and help me return the chairs to the rental company on Monday, I'll pay you the same rate I would have paid Steve."

I glanced at the hearse parked on the curb. "I was going to sell it," I said slowly.

"Why? It's such a convenient vehicle! Getting these chairs moved was dead easy with that hearse." Marlee laughed. "No pun intended."

"Yeah, it was easy," I said, a new and possibly crazy idea popping into my head. "Dead Easy Delivery is at your service!"

TWELVE

MARLEE'S COMMENT HAD INSPIRED my business idea as well as the ridiculous name for it. Her giggle when I said, "Dead Easy Delivery" had convinced me it was the right thing to do. Sure, I could get a lot of money if I sold the hearse. But I would only get that money one time. If I started a delivery service, I would get a little bit of money on a regular basis.

If I can find customers, a little voice in my head reminded me.

So, with that in mind, I left the hearse parked on the curb, said goodbye to Marlee, and walked across the street to the Sit a Spell Tavern. The place was the busiest I had seen it, and there were no free stools at the bar. Valerian was bustling from one patron to the next, pouring drinks with smooth speed.

When I got closer to the bar, I stopped and was about to turn around and leave, figuring I could pitch my delivery service idea later, when Valerian wasn't so busy. But, when I heard her tell someone, "Sorry, I'm all out of that. We won't have any more until we find a new delivery person," I changed my mind. My services were needed, and if I wanted the job, I had to put myself forward.

I squeezed into a bit of vacant space at the end of the bar, where a young man was sitting on the stool Barry had occupied the two times I'd visited the tavern. I hated to think what would happen if Barry came in and found someone in his preferred place.

Valerian spotted me as I was trying to pull my elbows in as tightly as possible, worried I'd bump into the young man and send his beer flying. "Diet soda, or something harder for you today?" she asked as she hurried over.

"Neither. I'm here to ask if you'd consider hiring me as the new delivery driver."

Valerian gazed at me wordlessly, like she wasn't quite sure she'd heard me correctly.

"The hearse," I explained. "I was going to sell it, but as it turns out, it's great for hauling things. I thought I'd start offering my services around town."

Awareness spread across Valerian's face. "That's a great idea! Yes, absolutely, we will hire you. I mean, I have to clear it with Will first, since he owns this place, but that won't be a problem. Are you free to do a run tomorrow morning?"

"Sure."

"If we leave early enough, I can go with you and help you get acclimated." Valerian gave me a sly look. "I'm nearly done packing up my apartment, but I'd much rather hire you and your hearse than harass all my friends to help shuttle boxes to the funeral home."

"I'll give you the friends and family rate," I said with a wink. I didn't even know what my regular rate was, let alone the discounted one.

For that matter, I'd need a business license and whatever else came along with owning a delivery service.

That, I decided, could wait until later. I'd allow this first job for the tavern to be a trial run. If I enjoyed it, then great; I'd go ahead and turn Dead Easy Delivery into a formal business. If I decided hauling things around for people wasn't my cup of tea, then I'd sell the hearse and find some other way to make money.

I backed slowly away from the bar, still mindful of my elbows. By the time I reached the front door, I was grinning. I had two gigs for my brand-new delivery service: picking up the chairs after the wedding and doing a run for the tavern.

That positive feeling must have bolstered my courage, because the first thing I did when I got home was call my daughter, Tara. I had only talked to her a handful of times since I had moved back to Foxfire Haven. I was still getting adjusted to not seeing her a few times a week. But, as much as I missed her, things were currently strained between us.

"Hey, sweetheart," I said when Tara picked up. I was sitting at the table in the breakfast nook, one hand on my phone and the other cupped to give Perkins a spot to sit. "I'm just calling to check in and see how you're doing."

"Fine. Hailey has her preschool welcome party coming up this weekend." Tara paused, and even though she was miles away, I could picture the way her eyes must be sliding away, her lips twisting. It was the face she made whenever she was uncomfortable.

"She's going to have so much fun. Make sure to send me some pictures of her in that new dress you bought for it." I knew my own expression was similar to Tara's. Whenever we were both in a socially awkward situation, anyone looking at us would instantly know we were related. Missing out on Hailey's life was another one of the hard things about my move back to Foxfire Haven. It wasn't just my daughter that I missed.

I had heard the sound of the front door opening while we chatted, and as Tara was promising to send me both video and photos, Jo popped her head into the kitchen. She began to say something, then saw I was on the phone. She closed her mouth, waved, then disappeared.

"Are you happy to be using your magic again?" Tara asked in a strained tone.

"I haven't used it yet."

"Mom."

"I know. I will, eventually. I have to ease back into this." I sighed. "But it's not easy to feel confident when the town's chief constable thinks I might have killed someone with my magic."

"What? He called me to ask about you, but he never said...What do you mean he thinks you killed someone?"

"Didn't he tell you why he was calling?"

"He said he was doing a background check for something. I figured it was just a weird small-town thing, you know? The nosy neighbors wanting to make sure the newcomer was okay."

"I found a man in the garage behind the funeral home. He was dead. Murdered." I bent forward until the tip of my nose made contact with Perkins. He cooed quietly, and I felt a wave of calm emanating from him. It gave me the steadiness I needed to bring Tara up to speed.

When I was finished, Tara was silent. Eventually, she said, "I'm so sorry this is happening to you, Mom. I wanted it to be easy for you. I thought you'd be happy there."

"I'll get through it," I said, forcing myself to sound confident. *Of course I'm not happy here*, I wanted to say. *I can't see you or Hailey all the time.*

I even missed my son-in-law, Brian, even though he and I had never become particularly close.

Before I could let my resentment and sadness show, I ended the call. I put down my phone and lifted Perkins to my chest, snuggling him against me.

"Hazel?"

I looked up to see Jo in the kitchen doorway. "I wasn't trying to eavesdrop, but that didn't sound like a very fun call."

"I was checking in with my daughter," I said. "Things are, ah, a bit tense between us at the moment."

Jo gave me a sympathetic look. "No amount of magic can fix a relationship. I hope it gets better."

"I hope so, too."

"I'm heading to dinner with some of my friends from book club. Why don't you come along? They would love to meet you."

I thanked Jo for the invitation, but I told her I was looking forward to a quiet evening. I should have been heading to the magic store to talk to Adeline Beaumont, but after that conversation with Tara, I was feeling deflated. I had been so excited about my delivery service idea earlier in the day, but no matter how hard I tried to cheer myself up, I went to bed in a slump.

The next morning, I had to get up earlier than usual so I could be at the tavern by eight o'clock. Valerian had asked me to meet her there so we could load up some empty crates that needed to go back to the beer and liquor distributor over in Stanton.

I was yawning as Valerian and I slid the crates into the back of the hearse, but I didn't feel bad, because Valerian was doing the same. *At least she's not a morning person, like Jo.*

"Think we can squeeze this thing through a drive-through?" Valerian asked as we hit the road. "There's a place with good coffee near the highway."

"How about we just go inside and order, instead?" I suggested.

So, after we grabbed coffees, I eased the hearse onto the highway and headed south. The motor growled less as I went faster: it seemed to enjoy being out on the open road. Several cars that passed us slowed as the drivers tried to get a better look, and Valerian and I waved at the people with delight.

The drive from Foxfire Haven to Stanton was only about thirty minutes long, and soon, I was off the highway and headed down a two-lane road. We passed several hulking factories and a sprawling junkyard before Valerian expertly guided me down side roads. The warehouse for the distributor was down a road that wound through some hills dotted with rain-soaked fir trees.

I backed the hearse into a loading bay, right next to several large box trucks. The hearse looked ridiculous next to them, which only made me laugh, and soon, the other drivers were gathered around the hearse, wanting to know all about it, including how well it could haul beer. I showed them the built-in rollers that had been used for sliding caskets in and out of the back, adding that they would work for loading beer crates, too.

A man joined our group, looking at the hearse with a mixture of amusement and surprise. "Valerian, you said it was going to be an unconventional pickup, but that didn't prepare me for this sight. Can I take a few photos?"

"Ask the owner of Dead Easy Delivery," Valerian said, sweeping a hand toward me.

I quickly agreed, and after the man, who introduced himself as James, finished the impromptu photo shoot, he called a couple of employees over to help unload the empty crates. As we worked, he asked why Steve wasn't handling deliveries for the tavern anymore, and Valerian broke the news about the murder.

"That's a real shame," James said, without sounding like he really felt the sentiment. "I hate to say it, but I'm not going to miss that guy."

I had shown up to do a delivery job, but I suddenly saw my opportunity to learn a bit more about Steve and why someone might have wanted him dead. "Did you also get frustrated by his unprofessional attitude?" I asked.

"I never minded him being late or looking like he'd been wearing the same T-shirt for three days. He was nice enough." James shrugged. "It was his shady sales-man stuff that got to me."

"Salesman stuff?" Valerian sounded surprised. "If he had some kind of side gig going, he never approached me about it."

"He would try to talk me into buying things that always sounded like a scam. The last time I saw him, he was trying to get me to invest in a new beverage company. He called himself the company's distributor, and he swore the drink gave a person a better chance of finding love. *Special botanicals*, he said. As if I'd believe there was such a thing. That hustler was trying to pretend he had a magic potion."

James shook his head and chuckled, but Valerian and I exchanged shocked glances. Had Steve been trying to sell magical potions to the outside world? And, more importantly, had it gotten him murdered?

THIRTEEN

"WOULDN'T IT BE NICE if there really was a magic potion to help us in love?" Valerian asked. Her laugh sounded fake to my ears, and I hoped James wouldn't notice.

"I know that's a strange little town you all live in, but Steve wasn't being serious, was he?" James's brow furrowed.

"Whether or not Steve believed he had found a special blend of botanicals, as you said, is something we'll never know." I smiled at James. "It does sound like a wild scheme."

As we got the hearse loaded up, the conversation moved on to typical topics, like the weather. As soon as Valerian and I were on the road again, though, she said, "What was Steve up to?"

"And who else knew about it?" I glanced over at Valerian. "Could there really be a love potion like Steve was talking about?"

Valerian shook her head. "Not really. Sure, there are herbs that might help someone find love. Cinnamon for confidence, sweet clover for luck and a glowing complexion, and that sort of thing. But there's no magic that can make someone fall in love with you." Valerian reached over and put a gentle hand on my arm. "You know that, right?"

"I'm slowly remembering my magical chemistry lessons in high school. There's nothing that can create emotions, but there are things that can help create the right environment for those emotions to develop."

"Right. Just like my Good Mojo Martini. You can't really create luck, but my potion will enhance confidence and optimism, and people who feel good are likely to look at things in a more positive light. And when you're feeling positive, you're more likely to seize opportunities you might otherwise dismiss."

I nodded. "I remember Mrs. Nolan telling us in the fifth grade that ninety percent of magic is mindset."

"Intention is vital in magic," Valerian agreed. "But that leads us back to Steve, and what his intentions were."

"James said Steve called himself the distributor of this magic beverage. That implies other people were involved."

"He would have needed someone with an incredible knowledge of potions, because creating a drink that has magical properties and tastes good can be extremely difficult."

Valerian and I fell silent, and I knew we were both wondering who could have been behind the alleged love potion. My thoughts instantly turned to Adeline Beaumont, the owner of the magical supply store. Gnorris said he had spotted Steve making deliveries to her in the middle of the night, but maybe, Steve had been picking up an order of the potion rather than dropping off magical supplies. It was taboo to sell magical items to non-magical people, so anyone involved in the scheme would have wanted to keep it secret.

And, perhaps, someone involved in that secret had killed Steve.

I huffed out a frustrated breath as I merged onto the highway, heading north toward Foxfire Haven. "The division between our worlds has always frustrated me. The fact we stood there and laughed off the notion of a magic drink irks me. Why couldn't we have told James that, yes, a magical potion could be real?"

"You already know the answer to that," Valerian responded. "People get uncomfortable around witches, or vampires, or anyone who's different than the norm. Face it, Hazel, you're not normal. It makes me like you more, if that means anything."

"It does mean something. And you're right, I do know why we need to be cautious. I was naive when I left Foxfire Haven for college. I thought I could be a witch in the mundane world, as long as I was careful to keep my magic private. But, when my daughter was eight, she and her friends caught me working a spell for safety. It was for a road trip we had coming up, and Tara's friends panicked when they saw me. It was too strange for their little minds."

"And you stopped practicing witchcraft because you felt so bad," Valerian said. She wasn't asking a question. Rather, she said it with a calm, sympathetic knowing.

"I haven't touched magic since then. Tara begged me to quit because she was so embarrassed. I wasn't like the other moms, and that fact mortified her." I wiggled my shoulders, like I could fling off the sad memories. "How did you know I stopped practicing, anyway?"

When Valerian didn't answer, I looked over to see her staring down at her hands, which were folded tightly in her lap. Eventually, she said quietly, "Look, I know this is an awkward subject, but when Barry came into the bar that day, you...Well, um..."

I felt my cheeks warm. "Oh, no. I shed, didn't I?"

"Just a little bit," Valerian said quickly. "If it makes you feel better, I don't think anyone else noticed. Plus, your magic is a really pretty shade of pink!"

I groaned in answer.

"Hazel, you know you can't let excess magic build up inside you. It has to be released, or it's going to find its own way out."

"Yeah. It sure will." If I hadn't been driving, I would have curled up into a ball and cried. Magical shedding was downright embarrassing. It was the witch's equivalent of farting in public: everyone knew you couldn't control your magic.

Magical shedding.

Magical exhalations.

Magical farts.

Whatever anyone called it, the more unused magic built up, the more powerful it became when it finally escaped. Often, it happened during emotional or stressful moments, and it had the potential to be dangerous.

Which was why Wyatt Hightower thought I might be dangerous, too.

Valerian was kind enough to change the subject after that, and I was grateful she got me talking about my planned bathroom renovations for the funeral home rather than my avoidance of magic.

Once we got the delivery unloaded at the tavern, it was almost time for Valerian to open the place up for the day. She invited me to hang out for a bit, but I declined. I was too eager to learn more about Steve's love potion business, so I wanted to pay a visit to Jo. As a reporter, she was plugged into everything happening around Foxfire Haven, so I hoped she might have heard some rumors.

I found Jo sitting behind a cramped desk inside an even more cramped office. The Foxfire Haven Recorder had been in the same small building for decades, and Jo's laptop looked entirely too modern against the backdrop of burgundy wallpaper and dark built-in shelves piled with books.

Jo waved me into one of the two chairs in front of her desk. "How did your first delivery go?"

"Great. In fact, I got some interesting information about Steve Zillmann." Quickly, I told Jo about him seeking a non-magical investor for a magical beverage business.

Jo's eyes lit up at that, and she instantly grabbed a pen and began jotting down notes. "Ooh, that's dangerous. What else?"

I gave Jo all the details I knew, ending with, "I hoped you might have heard something about the business."

Jo tapped her pen against her notepad. "Nope. If Steve was really part of some business venture aimed at mundane customers, then the whole thing was kept under wraps."

"Valerian and I were saying it could explain the two a.m. deliveries Steve was making to the magical supply store. Or, rather, pickups."

"Adeline is a wicked potion maker," Jo agreed. "She's not a witch, but she's learned a lot of tricks in her hundreds of years as a vampire."

I had been putting off paying a visit to the store, but I couldn't do that any longer. I had to get up my courage and go talk to Adeline. What, I asked myself, was the worst that could happen? I'd already been caught shedding in public once.

It wasn't even lunchtime yet, though, so I wasn't going to march into the magic store right then and there. Instead, I went home, ate lunch, and got some things done around the house. Archer dropped by to continue working on the attic wiring, and I put another coat of paint on the wainscoting in the dining room.

I waited until after I had eaten an early dinner before I even considered heading back into town. Jo was coming in the door just as I was walking out of it. "There's some fog rolling in," she warned me. "Don't try to walk or bike in this weather."

So, instead, I drove my own car, figuring it would be a lot easier to find a parking spot for a compact SUV than a hearse. Even once I had made it to downtown, though, I continued to sit behind the wheel. It took a few minutes before I could talk my feet into moving.

Into the Cauldron was the only store still open on that stretch of road. The front windows had a soft golden glow, making the store look inviting, like it would be a cozy refuge from the damp, dark evening.

With that in mind, I strode to the door and walked inside, taking measured breaths as I went.

The store was absolutely jammed with glass jars, boxes with hand-written labels, and shelves that looked like they might collapse at any moment. The scent of herbs hit my nostrils, and I turned to sniff a bundle of dried rosemary on a nearby table.

"Good evening," someone called.

I leaned to one side, trying to peer around a display of dried flowers that had a sign that read, *Stock up on summer's harvest for your winter working!* A woman was arranging mismatched glass jars on a shelf, and I was struck by how beautiful she was. Her skin was flawless, its olive color contrasting with her long silver hair. High cheekbones and a slender form made her look like some kind of exotic fashion model.

The woman turned to me with pale green eyes. "Let me know if you need help finding anything."

"Thanks." With a jolt, I realized I had walked into the store without a plan. I had been so focused on simply making it inside the store that I hadn't considered what kind of questions to ask, or how to even broach the subject of Steve's murder.

I pretended to browse while racking my brain. I was also chastising myself because I realized it would have been smarter to call the constables and pass along the tip about Steve's elixir scheme. I had no business questioning a potential killer.

Still, I was there, and I wasn't going to give up. When Adeline passed close to me with an armload of lavender, I said, "I'm looking for a potion that can help me with love. Do you have anything like that?"

Adeline's eyes narrowed. "I have items to make a potion like that, but not the potion itself. I don't do the work for you."

"Right. Of course." I could feel my heart thumping in my chest. "I just hoped you might have something pre-mixed."

"You're new in town, aren't you? I don't know what the magic store was like in your old town, but here, I only supply the ingredients. You have to do the magic and the mixing yourself."

"Understood." *So much for learning anything tonight.*

There was a banging noise from the direction of the front door, and I instantly tensed, recalling Barry the Bigfoot's dramatic entrance into the tavern. But, when I turned to look, I saw Marlee, the wedding planner I had helped just the day before.

Marlee pointed at Adeline. "Give me everything you've got, right now!"

Fourteen

IS THE WEDDING PLANNER robbing the magic store? I thought wildly.

Adeline held up both hands. In a smooth voice, she said, "Calm down, Marlee."

Marlee opened her mouth to retort, then her face fell. She brought a hand up to her forehead and groaned. "Sorry. Oh, Addie, I'm so sorry. I just got off the phone with a client, and she was nearly hysterical. I wound up taking on her feelings."

Marlee lowered her hand and gave her body a violent shake. Sparkles of dark-red magic puffed out from her body, then fell onto the floor.

"Hey!" Adeline gestured toward the pile of magic on the carpet.

"Oh, it'll dissipate," Marlee said, her voice calmer. "Anyway, I'm—Oh, Hazel, the dead lady! I mean, delivery lady! I didn't even see you there. Don't worry, I won't need your hearse for this order. I'm only here to buy dried parsley."

Adeline looked from Marlee to me. "Hearse?"

"I inherited the Taylor Brothers Funeral Home from my uncle," I explained. "I've decided to start a delivery service, using the hearse to cart things around for clients."

"Do you have a card? I need a new delivery person now that Steve is dead."

"I don't have cards yet, but I can write down my phone number for you." *Another thing to put on the new-business to-do list.*

As I was pulling a scrap of paper and a pen out of my purse, Adeline said, "It's ironic that your business is going to replace Steve's, considering his body was found at your new home."

I paused, halfway through writing my phone number. Was I making myself look more suspicious by jumping in to fill the gap left by Steve? When the chief constable found out about Dead Easy Delivery, he would probably have some very probing questions for me.

I would deal with that when it happened. At the moment, I had a business contact to impress. "Just call me when you need a delivery," I said, handing the paper to Adeline. Her cold fingers brushed mine, and when she smiled at me, I could just glimpse the tips of her fangs.

Asking Adeline about a love potion hadn't gotten me anywhere. But, maybe, working with her could lead to a clue as to what she and Steve might have been up to.

Adeline told Marlee she'd work on getting all the parsley collected, promising it would be ready by the next evening.

"Thanks. This bride is determined to have the biggest, most perfect wedding ever, and she wants to make charm bags for the attendees. She figured a heaping dose of parsley in each bag would add to the celebratory mood at the reception."

Marlee and I left at the same time, after saying goodbye to Adeline, and I sneezed when I reached the sidewalk. I opened my eyes just in time to see a faint cloud of pink magic swirling around me before dissipating. I hadn't had so many of those exhalations in San Francisco. Being back in Foxfire Haven was raising my magic.

I turned sheepishly to Marlee. "Sorry about that."

Marlee waved a hand. "I just got empathy magic all over Adeline's carpet, so I know how it goes. Sometimes that magic just has to get out."

I nodded, appreciating that both Valerian and Marlee had taken my exhalations in stride.

"I talked to Jo earlier," Marlee continued. "She says you're still looking for one more renter at the funeral home. I've been asking everyone around town if they know of a place up for rent, but Jo is the first person to have heard of something. She says I should have read the classifieds."

I laughed. "Three people around town have mentioned someone was enquiring about a room to rent, but none of them could remember who it was that had asked. Stacy at the stationery shop mentioned it first, then my server at the Salt Circle, and Petunia at the garden store also brought it up."

"All places I frequent often. I get wedding invitations made at Stacy's, Petunia designs the best bouquets, and Karla over at the cafe makes the most divine cakes." Marlee sighed. "No one ever remembers me, just the events I put on."

"Honestly, I don't know how. I found you very hard to forget."

Marlee's face lit up. "Thank you. I'll call you about that room. In the meantime, I'm going home to do an energetic clearing spell. This client is just so high-strung, and I can feel some of her energy still floating around in my system."

"Good luck."

I headed home feeling good. I hadn't gotten any useful information out of Adeline, but I had possibly gotten my third renter and a new delivery service client. The idea of the funeral home's old radiators filling the place with warm air was feeling like more of a reality.

Jo was in the dining room when I got home, papers spread out across the table in front of her.

"Working late?" I asked.

"Working magic. This is everything I've written down in the past three months, and I'm going through it all to see what worked and what didn't. For example, I got my laid-back room here. In another misfire, I wrote at the beginning of July that I wanted some peace and quiet because I was feeling overwhelmed with work. The guy I was seeing disappeared for two weeks around that time. Not the kind of peace and quiet I had wanted."

"I take it that, unlike Steve, he showed back up, alive and well?"

"Alive, at least." Jo blew out a breath. "Dating is such a pain, isn't it? I'm too old to be doing this."

"I went on three dates after my divorce. All of them were terrible, and I swore off men forever." I reached out and gave Jo's shoulder a squeeze. "But I think it's nice you're still out there, looking for a special someone. Who knows? Maybe you'll inspire me to give it another try."

Jo huffed out a laugh. "I don't recommend it. I think I'm going to take a cue from you and enjoy being an unattached, independent woman."

"If Marlee takes the third room, we'll have a houseful of amazing women," I said confidently. "Thanks for letting her know I've still got a space open."

Before Jo could respond, there was a loud braying noise, and I felt a rush of wind ruffle my hair. Gordon had swooped into the room, and he came to rest on one corner of the table.

Jo nodded toward him. "He's one of the reasons I was happy to invite Marlee to move in here. Gordon and her familiar get along great. I think Perkins will approve of Stella, too."

"I'm glad to hear it." I left Jo to her review of her manifesting magic and headed for the kitchen. As I was loading dishes into the old dishwasher, my phone buzzed, alerting me that I had a text message.

It was from Archer, who said he would arrive in the morning to finish up the attic wiring. *Should I also replace those old sockets near the workbench in the garage?* he added.

Sure, I typed.

It wasn't until I had sent my reply that I got a prickle on the back of my neck. The garage had been locked when I moved in, and I certainly hadn't let Archer in there. But, if he knew where the sockets were and that they were in need of replacement, that meant Archer had been inside the garage at some point.

When had Archer been inside my garage?

And, more importantly, why?

Fifteen

I PUT MY PHONE down slowly, wondering if Archer was a suspect in Steve's murder. I'd seen him going into the tavern one day, when I had been on my way out. He and Steve might have known each other from there. Or, in a town as small as Foxfire Haven, they likely knew each other just from working with the same people.

My phone buzzed again while I was prepping the coffee maker for the next morning. It was Marlee, telling me she would be moving her belongings in the following day. She wasn't even going to look at the room first, and I wondered what her current living situation was that she was so eager to get out of it.

Then, right as I was wrapping up in the kitchen, Valerian called to confirm she would have time to move her things the next morning. "Can you please bring the hearse to my place? Between your hearse and my car, we can get most of it done in one trip."

Valerian gave me her current address, and I promised to be there at eight o'clock. For two women who weren't morning people, we sure were meeting up at early times.

I woke up the next morning feeling excited. Even though I still wasn't enthusiastic about having a houseful of roommates, I was looking forward to getting those three rent checks every month. I ate a quick breakfast, then gave Perkins a pat on the head. "You're going to meet some other familiars today," I told him. "I hope you like them."

Perkins hooted softly, rubbed his face against my hand, then snuggled down into his flannel nest.

By the time I pulled the hearse up in front of the small apartment building Valerian was living in, she had already piled cardboard boxes on the sidewalk outside. As we loaded them into the hearse, she explained that her landlord was hiking the rent. Her lease was up at the end of that month, so my search for roommates had been perfect timing for her.

"Besides," Valerian added, "I'm hardly ever home, anyway. Most of my life is spent at the tavern. I don't need an entire apartment to myself."

A massive raven fluttered down onto the roof of the hearse. It clicked its beak and cawed loudly.

"You're right, Lonnie," Valerian said. "You live there, too. But I think you'll like it at the old funeral home."

The bird cawed again, then spread its black wings and launched into the air.

"Your familiar, I take it," I said.

"She can be a bit temperamental, but you'll get used to it," Valerian assured me. "My ex-husband said Lonnie and I are a lot alike. We're both loud, opinionated, and bossy. I told him I took it as a compliment."

"I see why he's your ex," I intoned.

Once both the hearse and Valerian's car were loaded up, it was time to head back home. The only things that hadn't fit into our vehicles were Valerian's bed and a small table with two chairs, but she assured me it was no problem. The owner of the tavern had a pickup truck, and he'd help her bring the larger furniture over before it was time for bed that night.

When I pulled into my driveway, I slowly rolled to a stop before reaching the funeral home. A limo and a firetruck were both parked in the circular driveway.

My first instinct was to feel panic since the fire department was at my house. But, when I saw two men pulling boxes out of a compartment on the side of the truck, I realized Marlee had recruited some very unusual help for getting moved in.

I eased onto the gas pedal, pulling up behind the fire truck. Marlee caught my eye and gave me a wink over the top of a large box she had her arms around.

Valerian and I had just begun to unload the hearse when Marlee came up to us. "Jo told me which room is mine. That stained glass is lovely!"

"I'm glad you like it," I said. "I still can't believe you rented the place without ever seeing it."

"It's not about the place; it's about the people. I've known Jo for years, and you were kind enough to stop and help a stranger with a chair problem." Marlee reached a hand toward Valerian. "And I've seen you at the tavern, but we've never met formally. Do you ever do freelance bartending? I'm always looking for someone to serve drinks at wedding receptions."

Valerian looked Marlee up and down, like she was sizing her up. Then, with a satisfied nod, she said, "I'm open to freelancing once in a while. You did Artie Sullivan's wedding, right? It was beautiful."

"Artie and Amanda were great to work with."

Two firemen were carrying a small dresser up the front steps, and I hooked a thumb in their direction. "I didn't know the fire department doubled as a moving service."

"The fire chief was recently married, and he was really happy with how well I pulled off the whole thing, despite some rainy weather." Marlee waved toward the limo. "And I give J.T. a lot of business, so he was happy to help, too."

Valerian laughed heartily. "Between you making connections at events, me having a bunch of regulars at the tavern, and Jo being a reporter, we probably know everyone in this town. That's good, since we have to help Hazel settle in and get herself a social life."

I reached into the back of the hearse and grabbed a box. "Not just yet! I need to get the funeral home fixed up first, and then I can think about going out and having some fun."

The morning sped past. Even though the task of shuttling boxes into the former chapels was tedious, the banter and laughter kept things light. By the time the last box had been moved, the firemen had invited all of us to stop by the station sometime for a tour.

I made a lunch of chips and sandwiches for everyone as a thank you. The dining room table was certainly getting some use lately, and we all just managed to squeeze around it. Once we were finished eating, Valerian left for her shift at the tavern, and the limo driver and firemen headed out.

Once it was just Marlee and me sitting at the table, I asked, "What do you know about Archer Evers, the electrician?"

Marlee lifted a finger toward the back of the house. "I saw him out there doing a few things. He does good work."

"I agree. What I meant was, can you tell me anything about him as a person? Is he a decent guy?"

"I've never heard anything bad about him, but I don't really know him. Why do you ask?"

I didn't want to tell Marlee my worry that Archer might be a suspect in Steve's murder. After all, I had nothing to go on except a strange feeling and the fact that he had been inside the garage at some point. So, what I said instead was, "The guy is in and out of my house a lot, so I was just curious."

Marlee offered to help clean up the lunch mess, but I told her I could handle it. I was sure she was eager to start unpacking, and I didn't mind loading the dishwasher by myself.

During the afternoon, I would occasionally hear noises from Marlee's room as she worked, but I only saw her a handful of times. While she got settled in, I busied myself with the tile in the bathtub. It had been woefully neglected over the years, and it was going to take some serious scrubbing to get decades of limescale and soap scum cleaned off.

I was exhausted by three o'clock. Helping someone move and deep-cleaning an old funeral home bathroom in one day had been ambitious. After a short nap and a cup of coffee, I was ready to tackle much easier tasks, like folding my laundry.

When I heard Jo walking down the hallway—I was already recognizing her distinct footsteps, bold but not angry—I decided it was time to quit working for the day.

Instead, I went into the kitchen and started work on a salad. I wanted something quick and easy.

Jo walked in as I was slicing up a tomato. "Oh, perfect! I stopped and got some cucumbers and cheese on the way home. Care to combine forces?"

I quickly agreed, and the resulting salad was so enormous that Jo fetched Marlee to help us eat it. The three of us opted to sit in the breakfast nook. It was already dark outside the window, and when I saw a white blur go past, I said, "Gordon is on patrol."

"He and Perkins have been showing that raven around," Jo said.

"That's Lonnie, Valerian's familiar." I turned to Marlee. "Where is your familiar?"

"She flew off as soon as the firemen arrived this morning." Marlee shrugged. "Stella is rather shy, so she tends to stay away from crowds."

I laughed. "Valerian says Lonnie is a lot like her, but it sounds like your familiar is the opposite of you, Marlee. Your whole career is about bringing groups of people together."

"Wait a second," Jo said. "Are you telling me all four of us have birds for familiars?"

Marlee waved a forkful of lettuce around. "I realized that this morning. Stella is a toucan, believe it or not. A beautiful tropical bird, all the way up here in the Pacific Northwest."

We were still chatting when Valerian got home. She groaned as she plopped down into the empty chair at the table. "I was supposed to get off work an hour ago, but the late-shift bartender is terrified of my biggest customer, so I had to stick around until he finished his drinking and left for the day."

And, by biggest customer, I assumed Valerian meant in physical size rather than the size of the bill. I'd be a bit wary about serving Barry, too.

As Valerian helped herself to what was left of dinner, Jo sat back in her chair, a thoughtful look on her face. "There are four of us. Four witches," she said. "We can combine our magic to help solve the murder. My manifesting magic can help bring about answers."

"I don't have a truth potion," Valerian said around a mouthful of salad. She swallowed, then added, "But I am good at getting people to talk. I joke that being a bartender is just like being a therapist, but with alcohol."

"I can use my empathy magic to know how suspects are really feeling," Marlee offered.

"I'll grab my grimoire. I have a good power-boosting spell in there," Jo said. "We can do it first, to bind and boost our combined magic. There are four of us, which is just enough for a coven. We can call the four corners. We'll just have to figure out who's going to represent which element: earth, air, fire, water."

In unison, Valerian and Marlee said, "I'll represent air!"

Jo frowned. "But I'm always air in group spell-work. My familiar is a pelican."

"I have a raven, so I'm always air," Valerian said.

"And Stella is a toucan, and Perkins is an owl," Marlee finished. "All of us are used to representing the air element when we do group spells, because our familiars fly."

"Maybe we can take turns," Jo said slowly. "You know, we all rotate through the corners, so a different witch represents air each time."

Valerian looked at me. "It's your house, Hazel, so it's your call. Assign us each to a corner so we can work this boosting spell. North, south, east, and west. Earth, fire, air, water."

I had been silent the entire time, trying to sink down into my chair. But, as my three roommates looked at me expectantly, I knew I had to come clean.

"I won't be participating in the spell, anyway, so it doesn't matter to me."

All three of them protested, but Jo's voice rose above the others. "I know you said you haven't practiced in a while, but you have to start somewhere!"

"I haven't practiced magic in twenty years." I pressed my lips together and blinked my eyes rapidly, trying to hold off the tears forming in my eyes.

sixteen

"Oh, Hazel." Valerian reached across the table and put her hand over mine. "You mentioned you haven't used your magic since that slumber party your daughter had, but I had no idea it had been that long. Plus, I just assumed you'd be getting back to the craft now that you're in Foxfire Haven again. Isn't that why you came here?"

"Yes." I wiped at a tear on my cheek with my free hand. "I have to start practicing again, before it becomes a problem."

"Before you have another—" Marlee raised both hands, her fingers splayed. "Poof."

"Exactly."

"Oh, did you see Hazel's magic, too? Such a pretty shade of pink!" Valerian smiled reassuringly at me.

Jo was looking back and forth between Valerian and Marlee. "Hazel had another *what*? What are you all talking about?"

"A magical exhalation," I said. "My magic has spilled over of its own accord twice since I got back to Foxfire Haven."

"Then you definitely need to be practicing regular-ly." Jo slapped a palm against the table. "Use up that magic before it escapes again!"

"I know that's what I need to do." I sniffed loudly. "It's just...To be honest, I'm scared."

Valerian, Marlee, and Jo all looked at me blankly. The three of them had never walked away from their witchcraft. They had never tried to turn off their inherent magic.

And none of them had ever been through the hu-miliation I had experienced.

"I didn't move back to Foxfire Haven because I wanted to start practicing magic again," I began. I could feel my heart thumping wildly in my chest. I hadn't shared my story with anyone yet, and I didn't know if my roommates would be shocked, scared, or if they would simply laugh at me.

I took a deep breath before I continued. "As I told Valerian, when my daughter was young, her friends saw me working magic in the kitchen during a sleep-over. Two of them were so scared they called their moms to come get them. Tara was embarrassed, and she asked me to stop doing magic so I'd be a normal mom, as she put it. I haven't done magic since."

"Hazel, dear." Marlee gave my arm a gentle squeeze.

"But, of course, my magic would build up inside me since I wasn't using it," I continued. "I used to watch horror movies after Tara went to bed. I knew they would scare me, and that fear would trigger a magical exha-lation. I thought I was keeping things under control by shedding my magic when no one was looking. After Tara grew up and moved out of the house, though, I got a little lazy. A lot of magic built up."

Valerian winced. "How bad was it when it was finally released?"

"Bad. It happened the night of my granddaughter's dance recital. She's not even four years old yet, and you know how cute those little kids are in their pink tutus and tights." I smiled at the memory of Hailey twirling on stage, out of sync with the music, like the rest of her dance class, but still adorable. "At the end of the night, someone walked up to the front of the stage with a bouquet for the dance teacher. When the teacher walked forward to take the flowers, she tripped and fell off the front of the stage."

"And your adrenaline and fear both skyrocketed," Jo guessed.

I nodded. "I was in the second row, and I immediately jumped up to help. But as I stood, this wave of magic just ripped outward from my body. It was like someone had set off a pink smoke bomb in the theatre. The people closest to me, including Tara and her husband, were knocked to the ground, and the whole room vibrated. People panicked, thinking it was an earthquake."

I felt Marlee's hand on my arm again. Valerian still had her hand on mine, and then Jo's arms snaked over my shoulders. I took a few more deep breaths before I finished my story. "Tara knew what had happened, and she was horrified. She told me I was a danger to her daughter and to everyone in the mundane world. And, in that moment, I knew she was right. I could have hurt someone."

"You came here, where you could get back into the craft and not have to worry about earthquake-level exhalations." Valerian, I saw, had tears in her eyes.

I nodded. "I had inherited this place from Uncle Grant, but I had been avoiding having to deal with it. Suddenly, I saw it as my way to escape back into a world where I would be less likely to hurt people."

"You told me about Tara being embarrassed by your magic," Jo said. "But this explains why that phone call you had with her sounded so very awkward."

"I know she loves me, but she has to think of Hailey. Tara has to protect her daughter from me."

In answer, I heard a low squawk. I looked up to see Gordon perched on the kitchen counter. Perkins and Lonnie were next to him. A short distance away was a beautiful toucan. He had a black body punctuated by a white chest, and his yellow-and-orange beak seemed nearly as big as his body.

Perkins hooted, followed by caws from both Lonnie and Stella.

Despite how miserable I was feeling while recounting my story, I smiled. "Even our familiars are offering sympathy."

"Of course they are. They support us, like we support each other. And it's not just us helping you, Hazel." Marlee smiled sadly. "It's easy to feel lonely, helping all my clients get married and start a life together, while I'm always the single girl. Moments like this remind me that I'm not alone, after all."

"That's right." Jo looked around at all of us. "And we're going to help you rediscover your magic, Hazel. We'll help you ease into it. But, in the meantime, I'm still going to look up that magic-boosting spell."

"Thanks, ladies." I looked up at the familiars. "And thank you, my feathered friends."

Despite the discomfort of sharing my story, I went to bed feeling physically lighter, like a load had been lifted off my shoulders. Up until then, Wyatt Hightower had been the only other person in Foxfire Haven who knew what had happened to send me scurrying back to my hometown in shame. And, I wondered, just how much had Tara told him? Enough for him to believe I was dangerous, at the very least.

The next morning, I got a phone call just as I was finishing my breakfast. It was Petunia, the owner of the Growing Power Garden Store.

"I hear you and your hearse are for hire," she boomed. "I have a plant order that needs to go to the Watkins estate, out on the ridge by the coast. You available?"

Wow, word does travel fast in this town.

I quickly told her I could do it, happy to have landed a new client. Petunia and I agreed to my delivery fee, and she asked me to pick everything up at two o'clock that afternoon.

When I arrived, I found the plant order neatly arranged on the sidewalk outside, all ready for loading up. Petunia and another employee came out to meet me, and the three of us easily got everything into the hearse. As I closed the rear door, Petunia pulled a list out of her pocket and frowned.

"The order should have included two Autumn Frost shrubs, but I couldn't find them. I don't know where they've wandered off to."

"I didn't remember there being magical plants that could roam around town," I said.

Petunia didn't seem to know if I was joking or being serious. Her tone was a bit sharp as she said, "Of course there aren't plants like that. What a silly idea. It's a pretty plant, though, with bright red flowers in the fall. As the flowers fade, the tips of the leaves turn white. Of course, it's got magical properties, too."

"Oh, I have a bunch of those bushes in my backyard," I said. The red flowers were just tiny buds at the moment. "I had no idea they were magical."

"Sure. The next time you need to do a spell of noticing, it's a great enhancer."

I didn't bother to tell Petunia that I wasn't going to be doing a spell of noticing anytime soon. I'd been noticed quite enough the evening of Hailey's dance recital. Still, knowing I had Autumn Frost in my yard made me wonder what other magical plants might be growing around the funeral home. Cataloging them sounded like a nice way of easing back into my witchcraft.

Petunia didn't need to give me directions to the Watkins estate. Even though it had been so long since I had left Foxfire Haven, I still knew where the place was. It occupied the highest spot on a tree-covered ridge, the front of the massive three-story brick home looking toward the Pacific Ocean just a mile away.

My parents had retired to Port Onyx, a magical town in Florida that was full of old witches and other supernatural creatures, years before. My mom still lived there, and I made a mental note to tell her I got to visit the famous estate.

Before I could get onto the property, though, I had to use the callbox next to the ornate wrought-iron gate. A scratchy voice told me to pull around to the service entrance at the back of the house.

The man who met me at the service entrance started laughing as soon as he walked out of the door and spotted the hearse. "This is unusual!" he said. "We can put the plants here, next to the house. They're heading for different spots on the grounds, so I'll shuttle them around later."

As we unloaded the plants, the man's smile faded. "It's a shame about Steve," he said. "I have to admit, though, he started getting a little strange."

I immediately thought of my uncle, and what Roscoe and Holman had both said about him getting a little strange, too. "How so?" I asked casually. "I never met him."

Except after he was already dead.

"He said he'd be out of Foxfire Haven and on to bigger things soon." The man hitched up a shoulder. "He kept talking like he was about to come into some money, and he started acting cocky. Like he was too good to be delivering plants to the finest estate in the region."

Steve, I suspected, had been thinking of his magic potion business when he implied he'd be moving on to bigger things. Had he expected wild success by selling magical things to non-magical people?

Even if Steve had thought he was above delivering plants to the Watkins estate, I sure wasn't. The man gave me a tip in the form of a bottle of wine from the estate's vineyards, which I happily accepted.

Then, on my drive back to town, Valerian called to tell me there were a lot of leftovers following a company lunch the tavern had hosted that day. She suggested I stop by for an early dinner.

Free wine and a free meal, all in one day? I could get used to this.

Valerian said Marlee would head over, too, and we could pack up some food to take to Jo at the newspaper office. But, when I made it to the tavern, there was no sign of Marlee yet. I looked around, wondering if I should grab a booth or perch on a barstool, when I caught sight of Archer sitting in a booth with Roscoe. They were leaning over the table, their heads close together as they had what looked like an intense discussion.

Archer and Roscoe must have felt my eyes on them because they suddenly stopped talking and slowly turned to look at me. Roscoe glared, but Archer's face paled.

He looked like I had just caught him doing something wrong.

seventeen

ARCHER AND I CONTINUED to stare each other down, until he seemed to shrink into the back of the booth. His shoulders sagged, and, after a quick glance at Roscoe, he waved me over.

I walked to the booth and stood there with my arms crossed, looking down at Archer. His face was no longer pale. Instead, red was spreading across his cheeks.

"Whatever you're thinking, you're wrong," Archer said. I could hear the fear in his voice.

I was thinking that Archer and Roscoe might have killed Steve. Archer had been inside my garage at some point, even though I'd never asked him to go there, and even though the doors had been locked when I had first moved in. I didn't know why Roscoe was involved, but I was still inclined to think he would gladly plant Steve's body in the garage to further tarnish the Underwood name.

"Please, sit down," Archer said.

"I'll stand, thank you," I answered crisply.

"I should have been honest with you."

Roscoe made a sound in his throat that was almost a snarl. "I can't believe you're going to tell her."

Archer ignored Roscoe. "The two of us have been scouring the funeral home property for...Well, we don't know for what. Grant Underwood once told Roscoe there was something there, something valuable. We searched what we could without breaking and entering, but we didn't find anything."

I looked at Roscoe. "You and Grant used to be good friends."

"Yeah, until he started to change. He ruined a life-long friendship with his strange ways." Roscoe was scowling.

"You're the second person to mention it, but no one can tell me exactly what was going on."

"I'm not giving you a family history lesson today. Ask your own people."

"Sorry, Hazel," Archer said, looking pointedly at Roscoe. "Anyway, we have no idea what this valuable thing is, or where it's hidden on your property. What we do know is that Grant mentioned it to others, too, including Steve Zillmann."

"Do you think Steve was murdered because he was on some kind of treasure hunt, and someone else wanted the valuable item enough to kill for it?" And, I wondered, if that valuable thing was still on the property somewhere, then did that mean my own life was in danger from treasure hunters?

"We don't know," Archer admitted. "But it's something we have to consider. I told Roscoe we should go to the constables with this information, but he says we shouldn't."

"And why not?" I asked, even though I thought I already knew the answer.

Roscoe shrugged languidly. "Because they'll tell us to stop looking for the item."

"I'm telling you to stop looking for the item. I'm not upset that you looked around there while the funeral home was vacant, but that's where I live now. I don't want people trespassing, looking for some mysterious object."

"I haven't been out there since you moved in," Roscoe grumbled.

"And you," I said, rounding on Archer. "Were you really fixing the wiring in the attic, or were you looking for the item up there?"

Archer's face flushed even more. When he spoke, I could barely hear him. "I really was working in the attic. I looked around a bit, but the space is mostly empty."

I realized I was clenching my jaw, and I forced myself to relax. I couldn't blame Archer for his curiosity, and if neither he nor Roscoe had trespassed since I moved in, then I wasn't worried they were going to start. My anger didn't ebb entirely, but I also wasn't going to run to the constables to press charges.

"Who else did Grant tell about this valuable item?" I asked. "Other than Steve, I mean."

Roscoe and Archer exchanged a glance. "That's something the two of us are wondering, too," Archer said. "If we find out, we'll tell you."

"I would appreciate that." I turned and walked over to the bar. The stools were mostly occupied, and I wound up only three stools away from Barry. He was, as usual, hunched over a glass of whiskey.

"Let me mix these drinks, and then you're going to tell me what just happened over there," Valerian said as she hustled past on the other side of the bar.

A few minutes later, Valerian was back. She rested both hands on the bar and leaned toward me, scrutinizing my face. "You okay?"

I told Valerian about the bizarre rumor that Uncle Grant had been convinced there was a hidden treasure of some sort on the funeral home's property. In response, Valerian stared at the row of booths for a long time. "I think I remember that rumor. I was working one night, and someone said something about the funeral home having more than just dead people in it."

"Grant started talking about the hidden item after he began to change." The rumbling voice that spoke came from my right, and I swiveled slowly on my stool to find Barry gazing at me with golden-brown eyes that were only slightly darker than his fur.

"Everyone keeps telling me Grant started acting weird. What happened to him?" I had felt a spike of fear about having a conversation with Barry, but the look in his eyes was sympathy not malice.

Barry looked down at his glass as he twirled it in his fingers. "He started pushing away all of his friends. He thought we were all going to betray him, though none of us understood what he was talking about." Barry lifted the glass, drained it, then looked at Valerian. "One more, please."

I wanted to ask more questions, but Barry hunched over his refilled whiskey glass, clearly finished talking to us. I wasn't sure what surprised me more: learning that

Grant had been friends with a Bigfoot, or that Barry had actually spoken to me.

"You know who you should talk to," Valerian said.

"Jo." I nodded. "If she doesn't remember the rumors, there might be something in the newspaper archives."

Valerian made a shooing motion. "See you later."

I waved as I slid off the barstool. I even called, "Thanks, Barry" as I went, though I wasn't sure he was paying any attention to me.

It was convenient to have the tavern and the newspaper office so close to each other. It made it easy for me to visit my roommates. Soon, I was standing in the doorway of Jo's cluttered office. She was typing away on her laptop, glancing every now and then at a notepad that had scribbled writing all over it. I stopped and watched, not wanting to interrupt.

Jo was so absorbed in her writing she didn't notice me for a full minute. When she did, she gave a start. "Whoa! Hey! How long have you been there?"

"Not long. Do you have time to talk?"

Jo waved me inside the office. "Come on in."

As I complied, I asked, "What did you know about my uncle?"

"Grant Underwood? I know he was the funeral director here in town for decades."

"Yes, but did you ever hear rumors about him? People keep telling me he changed. That he pushed his friends away and got kind of strange."

Jo clasped her hands together on the desk. "I assumed you knew since he's your family."

"I don't know anything."

Jo sighed. "You'd better sit down."

EIGHTEEN

"YOUR UNCLE DID GET strange," Jo said as I sat down. "Most of this town knew him, of course. He dealt with all of our families at one point or another, as grandparents and other loved ones died. Grant was a good guy. The kind of person you trusted to treat everyone—the living and the dead—with compassion and respect."

"There's a 'but' coming, isn't there?" I asked.

"He started to change. This was a while back, maybe ten years or so. He became erratic, sometimes acting like the nicest guy in the world, like the Grant we all knew. Other times, he seemed angry, and I know some people worried he might turn violent, though I don't believe he ever actually tried to hurt anyone."

I sat back in my chair, guilt making my stomach feel heavy. I'd fallen out of touch with Uncle Grant after I left Foxfire Haven. I had sent a Christmas card every year, and sometimes, I'd get one back, but that was it. I had been shocked to learn Grant had left his funeral home to me. "It sounds like his mental health was declining. Maybe he had dementia."

Jo shook her head, her braids dancing around her face. "No. My grandpa had Alzheimer's. This was different. I know dementia can make people more aggressive, but Grant's behavior was more sinister than that. He wasn't like a man whose mind was going. I think it would be more accurate to say he was like a different man, entirely. Honestly, I think the whole town sighed in relief when he died."

I frowned. "If he was so obviously struggling with his mental health, why didn't a friend take him to a doctor? Didn't anyone try to help him?"

"I used to know someone who was friends with Grant. According to him, they did try to help. A few of them went so far as to cart Grant all the way to a specialist in Seattle, but no one could find anything wrong with him."

"How strange." And, I thought, how sad for Uncle Grant. After being such a big part of the community, and so well respected, it was a shame his life had taken a turn that ruined his reputation and alienated him from everyone. "Have you ever seen someone else act the way Grant did in his final years?"

"No. In fact, I didn't see Grant acting that way, since I rarely saw him. Most of what I know is from what others have said."

"Like Roscoe." I made a noise of disgust. "He and Grant were good friends, and now Roscoe talks about him with such disrespect. If it was just Roscoe who had told me about this, I would have chalked it up to him being a mean old man who doesn't like anyone. But then Holman mentioned it—Grant actually banished him for ten years—and then, just now, the Bigfoot at the tavern brought it up."

Jo half-rose from her chair. "A Bigfoot? At the tavern?"

I nodded, and Jo gave a little laugh as she sat back down. "You've been back in this town for only three weeks, and you already befriended a Bigfoot?"

"Hardly! In the few times I've seen him at the tavern, Barry just sits there and stares into his whiskey glass. Today was the first time I've heard him utter a single word. Valerian says he's in there every day, brooding."

Jo was quiet for a moment, then she sighed heavily. "I'll ask some of the old-timers I know what they remember about Grant. In the meantime, I really need to get back to work. My deadline is looming."

"Of course. I'll head back to the tavern for my free lunch." Even as I stood up, Jo was already positioning her fingers over the keyboard. "Thanks. I'll see you tonight."

I didn't think Grant's erratic behavior had anything to do with Steve's murder, but I still thought the rumors about something valuable being on the funeral home property might. I could just picture locals going out there, hoping to get rich, and getting into a scuffle with each other.

Part of me considered stopping by the constable station, so I could ask the chief constable what he knew about the rumors. I quickly discarded that idea, since I was still loathe to talk to Wyatt. If he had heard about the treasure, or whatever Grant had been looking for, then he was probably considering it as a motive for murder already, and I should just trust him to do a thorough investigation.

That afternoon, I was going through drawers in Grant's desk. The hulking piece of walnut was never going to leave the funeral home, as far as I was concerned.

It looked too heavy and too bulky to deal with, so I had adopted the office space as my own.

I had hoped to find something that might give me more clues about Grant's final years, but the only interesting thing I found was a yellowed cardboard fan with the funeral home's name stamped on it.

"That's from my day, you know." Holman was standing in front of the desk, looking appreciatively at the fan in my hand. "This air-conditioning thing you all have now wasn't around then. Not that it often gets very hot in Foxfire Haven, but I do remember a few August funerals that were sweltering. Some of the funeral attendees smelled worse than the corpse. Ugh."

"Uncle Grant thought there was a treasure hidden somewhere inside this building, or on the property," I said. "What do you know about that?"

Holman narrowed his eyes at me. "Treasure? Are we children playing pirates? There's nothing hidden in this place. I can walk through walls, lady, and I haven't seen anything hidden anywhere."

And, since Grant had banished Holman, the ghost probably never even heard Grant talking about his theory. I had known it would likely be a dead end, but it hadn't hurt to ask. I had to smile at Holman's reference to pirates, when I had so recently found the photo of my brother and myself dressed up as swashbucklers.

"Why are you here, Holman?" I asked suddenly. "You usually only pop up to make snarky comments about my appearance." I self-consciously lifted a hand to my cheek.

"You're in my office. That desk belonged to the funeral director before me. Hideous, isn't it? I would have chosen a desk with a little more style, but I didn't want to deal with moving this giant slab of wood."

I laughed. "I've had the same exact thought. Maybe you and I have more in common than I realized."

Holman raised his chin and smoothed a hand over his hair. "Perhaps. Though I'm still better-looking than you." With that, he disappeared.

When I heard a noise while mopping the wooden floor of the office a short while later, I didn't even bother to turn around. "Not now, Holman."

"That's the ghost, right?" It was Marlee, and when I looked, she was peering at the space above our heads. "Is he here? I haven't met him yet."

"Then that means he has nothing rude to say to you. You're lucky."

"Anyway, Jo and Valerian both called. Val suggested we do a confidence spell together. We thought that might help you."

I wanted to protest, because I was still afraid of working magic.

But if I don't start, more accidents are going to happen.

"That's probably a good idea," I conceded. "Maybe after dinner?"

"Yeah. I'm running out for a quick dinner meeting with a potential client, but I'll be back by eight. They're planning a family reunion, and those events are pretty simple, so we won't be at the cafe too long."

"See you around eight," I said.

I skipped dinner that night, too nervous about the confidence spell to eat. That decision was incredibly ironic and only served to show how much I needed the spell.

Jo got home before my other roommates, but she disappeared out the back door, saying she was going to explore the wooded area behind the funeral home. I nearly pointed out that it was almost dark already, but she had a flashlight in hand, and I reminded myself my roommates were adults who could take care of themselves.

Valerian and Marlee walked in the front door together, chatting about their respective days. I was just passing through the hallway on my way to check on Perkins when they came inside, and Marlee grinned at me. "You ready to do some magic?"

I just groaned in answer.

Marlee and Valerian decided we should do the spell in the backyard, since being out in nature would give us an energetic boost. As they laid out an array of candles and crystals in the center of the yard, I went through the house and called out to the familiars. "We're doing spell-work in the backyard," I said as I knocked on the doors for each of the rented rooms. None of them were locked, so I cracked the doors open.

No familiars came out to greet me, so I headed to the kitchen to collect Perkins, but he wasn't in his nest.

I walked out the front door and loudly announced it was time for the familiars to gather in the backyard. I heard the flapping of wings, and Lonnie swooped past, her black wings shining in the light from the front porch.

I let out a shriek as Gordon dove down toward me, his giant beak slightly open. "I am not a fish!" I called as he cruised past, close enough that I felt the whoosh of air in his wake.

Perkins landed on my shoulder. That was three out of four. "Stella?" I called.

Faintly, I thought I heard the click of a beak. I peered toward the oak tree in the front yard. "Stella, sweetie, are you in the tree? We're gathering in the backyard to do a confidence spell." I paused, then added, "It's for me, so I'll be more self-assured about working magic, but it will be good for you, too."

Some of the leaves in the tree rustled, and Stella flew into view. Instead of heading toward me, she disappeared over the top of the house. I turned my head toward Perkins. "She's still shy around all of us, isn't she? Don't worry. She'll settle in. You and I know what it's like to be in a new and strange place."

In answer, Perkins scooted closer to my face and rubbed the top of his head against my temple.

"Let's go get this over with," I told him.

When I arrived in the backyard, I saw that Jo had returned from the trees. Her pelican was perched on the top edge of the garage roof, with Lonnie settled in alongside him. Stella was sitting on Marlee's shoulder, gazing warily at the other birds.

"I suggest we skip calling the corners," Valerian said as she lit the white candles clustered together on the grass. "No point in another argument about who's going to represent the air element."

Stella's wings fluttered as Marlee shrugged. "We'll call each of the directions and elements together."

"Form a circle, ladies," Valerian instructed.

We complied, and I gave a nervous laugh as I linked hands with Jo on my right and Marlee on my left. "Not only have I not practiced witchcraft in twenty years, but I haven't practiced with other people in more than thirty years. I'm not sure I even remember what to do."

"Just follow along," Valerian said. "It will come back to you." Her white hair was down, and it seemed to shine in the light from the candles. She looked slightly ethereal, a far cry from the bartender I had met.

"North, south, east, west. Earth, fire, air, water." Valerian's voice was strong and soothing at the same time. Jo and Marlee joined in the chant, and I swallowed hard before adding my voice. After we had called out to the cardinal directions and the elements three times, Valerian said, "We stand here in nature, calling on the elements to assist us in our magical working. As we represent the elements, so do the elements help us work our magic."

Valerian dropped Jo's and Marlee's hands so she could stoop down and light a bundle of dried sage. As its smoke gave off a pleasant, earthy scent, she waved it over a large golden citrine crystal before placing it in a shallow bowl. Then, she stood and joined hands with the other women again.

"Now, we will recite the spell until we feel it has reached maximum efficacy," Valerian said. I wanted to raise my hand and ask how we would know that, but I kept quiet, trusting my roommates would figure it out for me. "I feel it growing, a powerful force radiating from me. I am confident in all I do."

Valerian began to repeat the spell, and the rest of us joined in.

To my utter surprise, I began to feel the spell working. A warmth spread through my chest, and I lifted my head toward the sky as a feeling of self-confidence grew inside me. "I feel it growing," I chanted, my voice louder than the others, "a powerful force radiating from me."

Suddenly, a wave of pink magic exploded from my body, sweeping across the backyard. Someone screamed, and beside me, Jo toppled over sideways, her fingers slipping out of my grasp.

Stella opened her beak and cried out as she took off from Marlee's shoulder.

There was a loud bang, and then everything went silent.

NINETEEN

"IS EVERYONE OKAY?" I asked in a shaky voice.

The first thing I heard was laughter. Jo was still lying on the ground, but in the candlelight, I could see her roll onto her back, her hands pressed over her stomach as she belly-laughed.

Marlee began to giggle, and even Valerian made a sound that was a combination of a sigh and a chuckle.

"I am so, so sorry," I said. "The spell was working, and I could feel my confidence growing, and then..."

"That was definitely a burst of confidence," Marlee said. She bent at the waist and blew on the still-smoking sage bundle, which was covered with a thin layer of my pink magic.

"Next time, we'll do a control spell instead of a confidence spell," Valerian quipped.

I turned toward the house. "What was that bang? I hope I didn't break anything."

The chairs on the back porch had all tipped over from the force of my magic. Jo and I began to right them while Valerian and Marlee collected the candles and other elements from our spell.

I had just righted the last chair when I heard Wyatt Hightower's voice. "Is anyone hurt?"

Wyatt was standing at one side of the backyard, looking around at all of us with an expression of genuine worry. Valerian quickly assured him we were all fine.

"It felt like a shockwave," Wyatt said, giving me a significant look. I knew then that Tara hadn't held back when she had described my magical incident at Hailey's dance recital. "I thought I should check on you ladies."

I averted my eyes, feeling embarrassed, and spotted a clump of my magic clinging to a leg of the chair I was closest to. I slowly rubbed my foot against it, trying to dissipate the magic before Wyatt could spot the little pink cloud.

Unfortunately for me, it didn't work.

"That's what I thought," Wyatt said, crossing his arms over his chest.

There was a loud hiss, and at first, I thought it had come from Wyatt. When the hiss was followed by the sound of hooting and cawing, though, I realized Wyatt's black cat had tagged along. The cat's back was arched and his tail was fluffed up to three times its normal size as he stared up at Perkins, Gordon, and Lonnie.

Suddenly, Stella swooped down low over the cat, dive-bombing from behind. The cat jumped and whirled around in a circle.

The other birds flapped their wings, like they were applauding Stella's bravery. She settled onto the garage roof, right next to Perkins, and the four of them glared down at the cat.

"Your familiars are trying to hurt Jazz!" Wyatt was eyeing the birds, his arms raised slightly like he was ready to fight.

"No, they're not," I said. "Your cat has been bullying Perkins, and Stella was just warning Jazz that his behavior will no longer be tolerated."

The sound of Marlee's renewed giggles broke the tension. "The confidence spell definitely gave them a boost."

"Confidence spell?" Wyatt asked.

Valerian told him we were trying to boost our confidence as witches, so we'd make a powerful coven. I wanted to hug her for framing it as a confidence spell for all of us, rather than singling me out as the one who needed the boost.

Even still, Wyatt seemed to know it had been about helping me. When Valerian finished, he rounded on me, one finger pointed at me in accusation. "You have to get your magic under control."

"And the only way for her to do that is to practice," Jo said. "If she doesn't use her magic, bad things will happen."

"Will happen? They're already happening." Wyatt gestured angrily toward the back edge of the yard, where even more of my magic was still clinging to an Autumn Frost bush. I really had made a mess.

"Give her a break," Valerian said. "She's a bit rusty after twenty years."

"And we're helping Hazel, so she's not alone in this." Marlee stepped onto the porch and took my hand. "She has her coven to support her."

Wyatt finally realized his threats were going to get him nowhere, so he turned on his heel and stalked off while grumbling about "lousy neighbors" and "feisty crones." Jazz slunk along in his wake, our familiars staring after him.

Marlee still had my hand in her grip, and she led me toward Valerian. Jo was on our heels. The three of them leaned in close and put their arms around me.

"It's going to be okay," Marlee said.

To my surprise, I laughed. "Maybe the spell worked, because I do feel confident! I'm confident it can't get any worse than that."

"Come on," Jo said, turning me toward the house. "The best thing after doing some wayward magic is a glass of wine."

Before long, we were settled in the living room, each with a glass of white wine in our hands. Our familiars had remained outside, flying off into the crisp night air.

Valerian and Jo both said a few choice words about Wyatt as we sipped, and I smiled contentedly. I had wished for this scenario just a week before, though in that version, there had also been ice cream.

The next morning, it was time to help Marlee return the chairs we had dropped off at the park. It was raining, and I was grateful for my raincoat as we loaded the chairs into the hearse. Once that was done, I drove the short distance to the rental company's warehouse, and we unloaded the chairs.

It was easy, quick work, and when Marlee asked how much she owed me for the job, I told her not to worry about it. "You stood up for me to Wyatt," I said. "That's worth more than any amount of money."

Marlee slung an arm around my shoulders. "He doesn't stand a chance against us. And, if you won't take money, at least let me buy you lunch. I'm chilled to the bone from being out in this drizzle. What we both need is the grilled cheese and tomato soup combo from the Salt Circle.

I readily agreed to that suggestion.

It was early for lunch, but The Salt Circle Cafe was already bustling. The hum of voices combined with the warmth made the space feel cozy and inviting, except for one thing.

Wyatt was sitting in one of the booths, sipping a cup of coffee.

His back was to the door, but I recognized his silver hair and the arrogant posture.

Marlee began to move toward a booth on the other side of the cafe, but I stopped her. "Order me that grilled cheese and tomato soup combo, please. I'll be right there."

I walked up to Wyatt's booth and slid onto the bench seat opposite him. He put his coffee mug down with a *thunk* and leaned as far back from me as he could.

What does he think I'm going to do?

I wasn't even sure what I was going to do. My feet had propelled me to the booth before giving my brain time to think about it.

"I want to apologize," I said.

Wait a minute. Do I really? Yes, I realized. I sincerely wanted to do this.

"I'm sorry my incident last night made you worry." I pursed my lips. "I know you weren't worried about me, but I'm sure you were concerned for my roommates and our neighbors. If I don't practice my magic, these things will keep happening. But it's going to take some work before I find my balance, magically speaking."

Wyatt grunted, then took a sip of his coffee.

"Did you know my uncle well?" I asked, moving on from my embarrassing moment.

Wyatt seemed surprised by the question. He put his coffee cup down again and gazed inside it for so long I began to think he was ignoring me. Finally, he cleared his throat and looked up at me. "You've been hearing stories from the locals."

"Yes. About Grant's erratic behavior, and his obsession with some valuable item he thought was located on the funeral home grounds."

Wyatt shook his head slightly. "That was never the Grant I knew. I saw him plenty of times over the years, and he was always a nice man. He'd keep candy in his suit pockets, and when kids got restless or uncomfortable at funerals, he'd slip them a piece with a little smile. I've heard the same rumors about his behavior as you, but I never saw it myself."

"And the valuable item?"

A server came by just then to refill Wyatt's coffee cup. He thanked her, his tone the friendliest I'd ever heard it, then shook his head again. "This is the first I'm hearing about that."

"I know a couple of locals were recently searching the grounds for the item, even though they don't know what it might be," I said. "I thought...Well, I wonder if that's why Steve Zillmann was in my garage."

Wyatt eyed me keenly. "You might be bad at magic, but you're decent at detective work. There's a possible connection there. As soon as I get back to the station, I'll make some calls, starting with these locals you just mentioned." Wyatt raised an eyebrow, prompting me to give up the names.

I hesitated. "I don't want to tell on them. I don't think either one of them killed Steve, but they didn't come to you with this information because they worried they'd get in trouble for trespassing."

Wyatt's eyes continued to bore into me, and I started to squirm in my seat. Finally, I relented. "Roscoe and Archer. They were talking about it at the tavern."

"Those two, huh? I'll drop by the tavern later."

Wyatt was still looking at me like he thought I was the killer. I might have come to the conclusion that he just had one of those faces—the kind that always looked grumpy and judgmental—except, just a few minutes earlier, I'd seen him flash a smile at the server.

Wyatt Hightower could be nice. When he wanted to be.

"Roscoe can be a bit difficult," Wyatt said softly. "He went through some tough stuff. Don't judge him too harshly."

I gazed at Wyatt. I'd been through something tough, too, and he was being pretty harsh toward me. Why did Roscoe deserve some grace, but I didn't?

I realized that if I continued to sit there, I was just going to work myself up. I didn't want to get into another tiff with Wyatt, so I said crisply, "Thank you for your time." I slid out of the booth as gracefully as I could manage and joined Marlee on the opposite side of the cafe.

Lunch was just as delicious as I had expected it to be, but I felt restless the entire time. My magic had probably started building up while talking to Wyatt, and the last thing I needed was another public exhalation. So, before going to the supermarket for a few items, I took a walk along Main Street. I'd learned long ago that physical activity was a good way to calm my mind and my magic.

As I passed the park in front of the town hall, I spotted a woman walking through the park in my direction. She was wearing what looked like a very expensive gray tweed pantsuit. Her glossy chestnut hair spilled over her shoulders in big fluffy waves, and it looked like it had been professionally styled. The woman's bright-red heels clicked against the sidewalk as she strode toward me.

The woman stepped right in front of me, and I had to stop to keep myself from plowing into her. "Oh, look, it's Hazie the Hag. I heard you were back in town."

My heart sank. "Euphoria Lachlan."

"It's Mayor Lachlan, and I thought this town was finally done with you and your weird family."

TWENTY

I FELT LIKE I was fourteen years old again. Euphoria Lachlan had grown older physically, but mentally, she was the same stuck-up bully she had been when we were kids.

With an effort, I forced myself to stand up a little straighter. "I see you inherited the job from your dad."

"I got elected because the people of Foxfire Haven love me," Euphoria countered. "You wouldn't know what it's like to be popular."

The Watkins estate was the grandest mansion in the area, but the Lachlan residence easily came in second. The family's house was a historic place a few miles outside of town, and I'd heard rumors that Euphoria's family employed a live-in housekeeper plus a cook, a gardener, and a nanny.

I wouldn't know for sure, since I had never been invited to the lavish birthday parties Euphoria had hosted every year back when we were in school.

If I don't get out of here, right now, my magic is going to explode out of me so hard it will knock Euphoria flat on her back.

I had to admit, there was something really tempting about that idea. But, if that did happen, then she would have yet another thing to bully me about, and it would only make Wyatt more confident I had accidentally killed Steve with my magic.

My teeth were clenched so hard I was liable to crack a molar. With as much control as I could muster, I said, "See you around, Euphoria."

"It's Mayor Lachlan," she spat back as I stepped around her and continued my walk.

As I kept walking, a new determination rose in me. I had been so afraid of practicing my magic again, but I wanted to show that snob Euphoria that I was tougher than she thought. I wasn't a teenager anymore, and no one was going to make me feel bad about myself.

It was time to face my fear and be a real witch again.

After I got some groceries, I headed home and instantly began the search for my old grimoire. I had packed it away decades before, along with some other keepsakes. Eventually, I found it in a beat-up box, underneath a pile of Tara's elementary school report cards, some photographs that showed a much-younger version of myself, and a silk bag containing my crystals.

I carefully laid the crystals out on the sill of the kitchen window. The sun was shining into the window, and it felt right to let them air out a bit after having been packed away for so long. Once they were arranged, I sat down at the kitchen table and cracked open my grimoire. The black leather cover had been embossed in gold, with my name written in the lower right-hand corner in a flowing script. *Hazel Underwood.* I was glad I had gone back to my maiden name after my divorce.

It was traditional for the parents of a witch to gift a grimoire on the witch's sixteenth birthday, and flipping through the pages of my grimoire was a fun trip down memory lane. The first pages were covered in big, carefully written cursive, and several of my fledgling spells revolved around typical teenage concerns. There was a simple spell to banish acne, and another one was what my teenage self had titled a "time-stretching spell," since it was designed to help get homework done at the last minute.

As I continued turning the pages, the spells—and the handwriting—had matured. Spells for success in finding a job or making friends with new people replaced the earlier subjects. At one point, I had created a spell for harmony in the home.

That one didn't work, I thought wryly. *I got divorced, anyway.*

On second thought, I realized I had felt a lot more harmonious after Nolan and I split up, so perhaps the spell had worked, after all.

There were no spells for making the town mayor stop being such a self-righteous meanie. However, there was one I had named Practice Makes Perfect. It was a potion that was drunk like a tea, and I had devised a chant to say in between sips. The spell had come about because I had once decided to take a knitting class, and after the first lesson, I realized I needed magical help if I was ever going to knit something more than a tangled mess.

But, in order to brew the potion, I had to use the right herbs. I needed to go back to Into the Cauldron, not to seek out a killer, but to stock up.

I was still mindful of the strong negative emotions I'd felt that day—first with Wyatt and then with Euphoria—so I walked to the magic store in the late afternoon.

If I still had a buildup of magic from my encounters with those two, I hoped the walk to town would help get it out of my system. I even wiggled my arms and hands as I walked, hoping to fling out any excess magic.

The sun was just setting when I walked into the store, which meant Adeline wasn't in yet. Instead, it was a young woman who was behind the cash register. She was staring at the screen of her phone, and she barely acknowledged my presence.

That was okay by me, though. I knew which herbs I needed, so I made my way through the store and collected them. When I dropped them onto the glass counter next to the cash register, the clerk finally looked up at me. "Just this stuff?" she asked.

"That's it."

It should have been easy, but it wasn't. There were no price stickers on two of the herb bundles, and the clerk had to go find the displays in the store to get the correct prices. It was a good thing I wasn't in a hurry.

Eventually, though, I was able to pay. As the clerk handed me my change, her eyes suddenly brightened in recognition. "You're the lady with the hearse."

"That's right. How did you know?"

"I saw you at the park with a bunch of chairs."

"Yeah, I was helping an event planner move them for a ceremony in the park. I'm starting a delivery service."

"Do you deliver people, too? Living ones, I mean. It would be such a cool way to go to prom."

I began to explain that the hearse didn't have a back seat, since the dead were always transported lying down. Before I could finish, though, I heard the front door of the store creak open, followed by the sound of Adeline's voice. "There is no other supplier," she was saying. "I had the only batch of the stuff, and that was the last of it."

My ears instantly perked up. Did this have something to do with the mysterious potion Steve had been hoping to sell to the mundane world?

Adeline sighed heavily. "I'm sorry, but that was it."

The call ended shortly after that, so I said my goodbye to the clerk and left.

Except, I didn't go very far once I got out onto the sidewalk. Adeline had told me she didn't have any pre-mixed potions, but if she was telling a customer she was out of a batch of something, that implied it was a mixture of ingredients. I wanted to know more, so I decided it was time to do a little spying.

I walked to the end of the block, turned right, and skirted around to the backside of the buildings that faced Main Street. There was a dumpster directly underneath a high window that looked in on the back room of the magic store, and I briefly considered clambering up onto it to peek inside. I quickly decided I was too old and too out of shape for anything like that.

The window, I noticed, was open. I didn't need to see inside. I just needed to hear. When I had flipped through my grimoire earlier that day, I had seen a spell of amplification. We had used it in high school to make our voices louder during football games, so we could cheer on our team.

Euphoria Lachlan had been captain of the cheerleading squad, of course.

Thinking of her further boosted my determination. I could use the spell to amplify my hearing, rather than my voice, so I could eavesdrop on Adeline. The only item I needed for the spell was lavender, and I had just purchased some of that for my Practice Makes Perfect spell.

"Remember the confidence spell," I whispered to myself as I pulled my bunch of dried lavender out of my bag. I selected two stalks of it and slid one behind each ear. Once I was positioned as close to the window as I could get without climbing onto the dumpster, I tried my best to ignore the smell of garbage and began to chant what I was fairly certain were the correct words.

It felt like the spell was working because there was a sort of tingling in my ears, but if Adeline was talking inside, I certainly wasn't hearing any of it. I began the chant again.

I was repeating the words for the sixth time when the tingling in my ears began to spread down through my entire body. It built up quickly, and I excitedly launched into a seventh repetition. My magic was working!

Then, quite suddenly, the tingling grew to a burning sensation. It was like that for just a fraction of a second, and then my body was surrounded in a ball of bright-pink magic that was expanding at a lightning-fast speed.

The explosion of magic ripped through the alley, and a car alarm began to whine. The lid on the dumpster flew open, slamming against the back wall of the magic store. My feet lifted off the ground from the concussion, and I landed hard on my backside in the middle of the alley.

I hadn't amplified my hearing. I had amplified my magic.

Before I could pick myself up off the ground, there was a bang followed by the sound of footsteps. Adeline's face came into view as I stared up at the night sky. "Are you okay?"

"I think so," I said hesitantly.

Adeline reached down and plucked one of the stalks of lavender from behind my ear. "What, exactly, are you doing back here?"

Twenty-one

I HAD LANDED IN a puddle, and I could feel my jeans soaking up the dirty alley water. There was nothing I wanted more in that moment than to sink down into that puddle and disappear. I stared up at Adeline, terrified. I needed to think up an excuse, fast.

"I haven't practiced magic in twenty years," I said, hoping to garner some sympathy. "I'm trying to start again, but the confidence spell backfired, and the amplification spell backfired, and I'm not sure I'm ever going to learn how to control my magic again."

Adeline frowned down at me. "Why were you practicing out here in the alley?"

"I didn't think anyone would see me," I answered. It was an honest answer, at least.

The young woman who had rung up my purchase earlier had come outside, too, and she pointed down at me. "That's the hearse lady," she told Adeline.

"Oh. You. You were in the store the other day. I thought you looked familiar." Adeline observed me coolly while I picked myself up off the ground.

"Sorry to have bothered you," I mumbled. Adeline was looking at me like she knew I had been up to something in the alley, and I wasn't going to try to convince her otherwise. At the same time, I wasn't about to explain myself. I turned and walked away, trying to look dignified despite a slight limp from smacking my right ankle against the asphalt.

I was grateful for the darkness as I made my way home. I was doubly embarrassed. Not only had my magic backfired yet again, but Adeline had caught me in the act of snooping around. The small flashlight I had stowed in my purse for the walk home remained there. I didn't want anyone to see my walk of shame.

It started raining halfway home, so by the time I reached my front door, I was wet through. I went right to my bedroom and changed into clean dry clothes. Once I had dried my hair, I wandered into the kitchen in a quest for some kind of sugary comfort food.

Marlee was sitting at the kitchen table. And, I noticed, Stella was curled up next to Perkins in the nest by the heater.

"Oh, no, Hazel," Marlee said. "What happened?"

I looked down at my fresh clothes. "How do you know something bad happened?"

Marlee gestured to herself. "Empath, remember? You are radiating sadness. You feel defeated."

"I had another magical exhalation, and it happened while I was trying to eavesdrop on Adeline Beaumont. She had been talking on the phone to someone about being out of a batch of something, and I hoped I might learn if she was referring to the love potion. But, my amplified hearing spell backfired, and she came running when I nearly annihilated the alley behind the magic store. She knows I was snooping around."

Marlee made a noise of discomfort, then jumped up from her chair and clapped her hands together. "I'm going to cheer you up! If I don't, I'm going to absorb your feelings, and we'll just end up on the couch eating ice cream and watching sappy movies."

"What's wrong with that?" I thought it sounded perfect.

"It's not productive. Stella, Perkins, come on. We need to support Hazel!"

The two familiars roused themselves instantly, and Perkins came to perch on my shoulder. He shifted his weight from one foot to the other, tapping against my collarbone. It was like a little dance, and it had always been his way of trying to cheer me up.

Stella opted for flying circles around my head.

Despite how dejected I felt, I couldn't help but smile at Perkins and Stella trying to lift my spirits. "Thank you, both," I said. "And you, Marlee."

"Oh, we haven't even gotten started yet. I've got something that's guaranteed to make you feel better."

That something wound up being a crumbling photo album. Marlee had left it on the dining room table, and she took me in there and told me to sit down. "I asked the historic society if they had anything related to this place. The photo album was the only thing they had, and they were kind enough to loan it to us."

I gasped with delight. "This is incredible!" I carefully opened the old album and saw a familiar face staring back at me. This time, he was in black and white rather than glowing. "There's Holman! Oh, wow, wasn't he dapper back then?" He was standing in front of the funeral home with two other people, a man and a woman, and he had his hands planted proudly on his hips.

The album must have been Holman's, because he appeared in many of the photos as I turned the pages. There were pictures of funeral displays, as well as many shots of the funeral home itself. I called Holman's name several times, hoping to share Marlee's find with him, but he never showed up.

Just as Marlee and I had finished looking at the photos, Jo came into the room. She had a plastic cup with a lid on it in one hand, and she held it out to me. "Val has to work the late shift, but she made this for you. She and I are sorry about your adventure behind the magic store."

I knew I was turning the same shade of pink as my magic as I asked how they already knew about it.

Jo laughed at my question. "The usual way. Someone who saw you in the alley told someone else, and they told someone who told someone, and eventually, word made it to the tavern."

"What's the drink?" I asked as I warily took it from Jo.

"Val calls it her Locomotion Elixir. It's for when you need to get moving, and she says you need to move on from this incident."

I removed the lid and took a sip. The drink tasted like an iced coffee combined with caramel and hazelnuts. It was delicious.

"And I'll write something to make you feel better," Jo offered.

I eyed Jo over the rim of the cup. Once I swallowed, I asked, "Do you think that's a good idea when so much of your manifesting magic goes awry?"

"Well..."

"I've got something better, and far less dangerous, to make you feel better," Marlee said. "Come on."

She led us out the back door and down the porch steps into the yard. It was still raining.

"I've already had to put on dry clothes once tonight," I said, wondering how this was supposed to make me feel better.

In answer, Marlee lifted both of her hands toward the sky. She said words that were too low for me to hear, but as I stood there, the raindrops stopped pelting my face. I looked up to see a small circular patch of clear sky directly above us. A few stars twinkled.

Jo and I both gasped in unison.

"You're a weather witch?" Jo sounded excited as her head swiveled from gazing upward to looking at Marlee with a newfound appreciation. "I thought you were an empathy witch!"

"I'm both," Marlee said. "It's why my event business is so successful. I can understand my clients' needs better because of my empathy, and if it's looking like rain for an outdoor wedding, I can make a clear patch. My weather magic won't hold for long, but if the wedding ceremony is less than thirty minutes, we're good."

Jo waved a hand. "If it's more than thirty minutes long, I don't want to go. Weddings should be fast, so everyone can get to the cake and dancing part."

"Agreed," I said, raising my Locomotion Elixir.

Between Marlee, Jo, and even Valerian, I did feel better when I went to bed that night. I figured Euphoria and Wyatt would both hear about the alley accident, but I didn't really care at the moment. Neither one of them liked me to begin with, so why should I worry about them disliking me even more?

Wow, I thought as I drifted off. *Maybe Valerian's potion really is helping me move on.*

I was just finishing buttoning a black cardigan over a green top the next morning when Holman appeared beside me. "No," he said.

"No, what?"

"That shade of green"—he pointed at my top—"doesn't work at all with that shade of lipstick."

I rolled my eyes. "What do you suggest? Should I change my shirt or my lipstick?"

Holman didn't seem to realize I was being sarcastic. Instead, he got a pleased look on his face. "I recommend you don't do either. Instead, put that darker red lipstick over what you're already wearing. The resulting shade will coordinate with the green, and it should make your lips look fuller."

When I ignored him, he wisely changed the subject. "I've been thinking about your uncle."

"And?"

Holman gave me an exaggerated wink. "Maybe I'm the valuable item he was looking for!"

"Except he banished you, so that's unlikely."

"I thought about that, too. Maybe he did it to keep me safe. By banishing me for ten years, no one could get their hands on me."

"Quite the theory," I said as I drifted out of my room.

There was a note sitting on the kitchen counter, just in front of the coffee maker. Valerian had gotten home from the tavern well after I'd gone to bed, and she had left a note asking if I could run to a nearby town to pick up a special order at a small gin distillery.

Since Valerian was still asleep, I scribbled *On it!* onto the bottom of the paper, so she would see it when she woke up.

After coffee and breakfast, I headed out to make the run. Getting out of town for a bit would be a nice break, especially since I figured I'd get strange looks anywhere I went in Foxfire Haven that day. In my mind, the entire town was gossiping about my exhalation behind the magic store.

The gin distillery was about a forty-five-minute drive away, all on winding two-lane roads that took me up and down the surrounding hills. It was damp out but not actively raining, and there were misty patches in some of the valleys I drove through. *Foxfire Haven might be the home of witches and other supernatural creatures,* I thought, *but this whole area feels magical.*

When I pulled up in front of the distillery, a man in worn jeans and a heavy flannel shirt came outside to meet me. "Valerian said I was going to get a kick out of the new delivery vehicle! Can I take a few pictures once we've got the gin loaded in?"

"Of course." *Part delivery service, part photo op,* I thought. *Maybe I should charge extra for pictures.*

The man went inside again and reappeared a few minutes later with six cases of gin loaded up on a rolling cart. He insisted on doing the loading himself, and as he began transferring everything into the back of the hearse, he said, "I was sad to hear about Steve. His poor son will grow up without a father."

I started. "Son? I didn't know Steve had any kids!"

"Yeah. I never met his son, but look at his adorable little hat!" The man reached into a pocket and pulled out a red conical hat.

It was clearly a gnome's hat.

Twenty-Two

THE MAN REACHED TOWARD me, the hat dangling from his fingers. "Can you please see that this gets back to Steve's son? I figured, in a town that small, you probably know how to pass it along to him."

I plucked the hat out of the man's fingers, trying to hide my shock. "I'll pass it along," I promised. Except, I wouldn't be taking it to Steve's son, since he didn't exist.

"It must have fallen out of Steve's truck the last time he did a delivery. I was going to give it back to him the next time he picked up an order for the tavern, but, well..."

But Steve had been murdered, and the only gnome in town had apparently been running around with him before he died.

Before I left the distillery, I texted my three roommates, telling them I had something I wanted to discuss and suggesting we meet for lunch. *See you in the kitchen at noon?* I typed.

By the time I rolled up to the tavern to deliver the gin, though, I had a string of responses waiting for me, which ended with the resolution to meet at The Woody Cottage at noon, rather than at the funeral home. I'd never heard of the place, but Marlee had suggested it, adding that it would be a free lunch for all of us. She apparently had a credit with the restaurant because she used them so often to cater events.

I couldn't argue with more free stuff. Being room-mates with Marlee and Valerian was going to save me money.

After the delivery, I headed home to get a few things done before it was time to go to lunch. Valerian had the day off, and I could hear her moving around in her bedroom, but I didn't see her until fifteen minutes before noon, when she came into the living room.

"You're dressed nice," I commented.

Valerian smoothed her flowing green skirt. Her long gold earrings glinted in the sunlight coming through the window. "Thank you. And before you ask, no, there's no special occasion. I like to dress up on my days off. That's all."

I glanced down at my outfit. "Do I need to change before we go to this restaurant?"

"No. The Woody Cottage is very casual. Can I catch a ride with you? I kind of like going around town in the hearse!"

I agreed, and as we drove, Valerian said she was dying to ask what this impromptu meeting was about. "But," she concluded, "you want to tell us all at once, and gauge our reactions."

"You're right. But, don't worry. I promise this isn't anything bad."

The Woody Cottage looked exactly how I'd hoped it would. It was situated right on the edge of the Foxfire Haven city limits, where there were few houses and a lot of trees. A dirt driveway wound through a wooded area, where the tall fir trees were so dense it felt like twilight beneath them, even though there wasn't a single cloud in the sky above. The drive opened onto a clearing, where a squat cottage with a slate roof sat. The brick exterior had vines of English ivy crawling up it, and there was an herb garden at one side.

The parking lot was behind the cottage, and it was nearly full already. Parking the hearse in a tight space was nerve-racking, but I managed to pull it off without door-dinging anyone.

Jo and Marlee were already there, standing near the back door of the cottage.

"I brought my notebook, in case whatever you have to share is something newsworthy," Jo called, waving a reporter's notebook in the air. "Or in case I need to manifest something."

"I don't think we'll need a story or an intention," I said, "but I am excited to get an opinion from all three of you on something."

We got the last available table inside the bustling little restaurant. The place must have once been someone's home, because instead of one big dining area, there were several small rooms that contained tables. We were ushered into a room that had leaded windows overlooking the herb garden. One of the windows was cracked open to let some of the fresh air inside. The only interior lighting came from candles burning in sconces along the walls and small tea candles on each table.

Once the four of us were seated, my roommates leaned their heads toward me. "What do you have to tell us?" Jo asked, her voice barely above a whisper.

"I picked up an order for the tavern this morning," I said. "It used to be Steve's route, and the man running the distillery said Steve had left something behind the last time he was there." I reached into my purse and pulled out the red gnome hat with a flourish.

Marlee sucked in her breath so hard she started to cough.

"There's only one person in town that could belong to," Valerian said. "Gnorris."

"This means Steve and Gnorris knew each other better than we thought," Jo said. "More than that, Gnorris was riding in Steve's truck at some point."

"But not to that distillery," I pointed out. "The owner thought the hat belonged to a child, and he figured it had fallen out of the cab of Steve's truck."

"Now, we need to know what Steve and Gnorris were up to, and whether it was anything that could have led to murder," Jo said. She had a pen in her hand, ready to take notes if needed, and she chewed absently on one end. "If Steve was involved in this secret love potion business, then was Gnorris a part of it, too?"

"I know one person in this town who can give us the answers," I said. "I'm going to drop by the garden store after lunch, so I can return this hat to Gnorris. After all, I promised I would return it to its rightful owner."

"I'll go with you," Valerian said. "I can pick up a pretty little succulent for my new room."

I winked at Valerian. "I'm glad to hear you're up for the visit, since I'm your ride."

The menu at The Woody Cottage kept with the homey theme of the place, and I chose a chicken pot pie for my lunch. As the four of us waited for our food, we moved on to other topics. Marlee told us she was trying to land a client who wanted an extravagant beachside wedding, while Jo complained about the lack of interesting news items coming across her desk.

"Your news is the most exciting thing I've heard all day," she told me.

"Let's hope this gets us one step closer to finding out who killed Steve," I said. "Then, you'll really have something interesting to write about. Have you heard any more bits of news about the murder?"

Jo sighed. "I've been trying. Chief Constable Hightower keeps giving me vague answers. However, when I politely suggested to him that the reason he wasn't telling me anything was because he didn't have anything to tell, he got the faintest look of panic on his face. I don't think the constables have gotten any good leads."

"That means we need to keep digging, too," Valerian said firmly. "If we don't learn anything today, then I'll ask a few pointed questions tomorrow at work. I have some regulars who are pretty plugged into Foxfire Haven gossip."

"And I have to go to the stationery store later," Marlee said. "I'll ask Stacy if Gnorris ever tagged along when Steve made a delivery to her."

Jo lifted her notebook. "And I'll keep an eye out for any news that might be related to the murder."

I left the restaurant, feeling optimistic that we would pin down Steve's killer before too long. I was eager for resolution, because I was still worried the person who took Steve's life might come back for me.

I blamed that fear on Wyatt, since he had put the idea in my head in the first place.

Even though I walked out of The Woody Cottage feeling confident, I began to feel nervous as Valerian and I neared the garden store. I told myself to calm down. I didn't think Gnorris had murdered Steve, so I wouldn't be confronting a killer.

Valerian suggested I should talk to Gnorris alone, so he wouldn't feel like he was being cornered by the two of us, but she promised to be nearby, ready to jump into action if needed.

She literally said "jump into action." I wasn't sure what that would entail or why I would need it.

We found Gnorris watering saplings in planters, so Valerian instantly dropped back and pretended to be extremely interested in a fern. I kept walking toward Gnorris, pulling his hat out of my purse as I approached him.

"You left this in Steve's truck," I said, holding it out toward him.

Gnorris jumped, letting go of the watering can. It clattered to the ground, sending water flowing across the concrete.

"What were you doing in Steve's truck?" Gnorris asked cautiously. Instead of taking the proffered hat, he stared at it like it might bite him.

"I picked up a gin order earlier," I explained. "The distillery owner gave me this, since it fell out of Steve's truck on his last trip there. I didn't know you and Steve were so close. Why didn't you ask him about his late-night dealings with Adeline yourself?"

Gnorris sighed as he reached out and took the hat. His head drooped so low the hat he was already wearing began to slip off. He adjusted it as he looked up at me with a resigned expression. "I didn't have to ask him. I was there when those late-night meetings happened."

"You told me you spotted the two of them while you were on your way home from the tavern."

"Because I didn't want to tell you the truth!" Gnorris's fist closed around the recovered hat. "The three of us were part of a scheme to sell a magical elixir to non-magical people. We'd downplay the magic, of course. Or, rather, I thought we would. Steve and his big mouth! He was actually telling people in the mundane world that the elixir used real magic."

I nodded. "He thought that would help sell it."

"That's what he told us, though Adeline and I were convinced people would think he was lying in an effort to make a sale. Outside people like to pretend we don't exist."

I bristled. I understood that magical people inside a magical town felt like they were in their own little world, but "outside people" had always seemed like a derogatory term to me. When I was growing up in Foxfire Haven, I hadn't understood why it struck me that way. Now, as an adult, I realized it wasn't the words themselves but the way they were said.

"Adeline could get all the ingredients easily," Gnorris continued, "except gelaroot. I know the grower since I work in gardening, so I could buy it from him under the guise of it being for the store. He would never think we were using it to brew an elixir."

"If you knew what Steve and Adeline were doing together on those late nights in the alley, then why did you tell me you thought Adeline was the killer?"

Gnorris had gotten a faraway look in his eyes, probably remembering the deals he had made for his part in
the secret business venture. At my question, though, his
attention snapped back to the present moment.

"Because," he said simply, "I do think Adeline murdered Steve."

Twenty-Three

VALERIAN WALKED PAST RIGHT then, pretending to be looking at plants. As soon as she was out of Gnorris's line of sight, she glanced back at me and raised one hand, her fingers and thumb formed into the sign for *okay*. Her eyebrows rose as she looked at me questioningly. I gave the smallest of nods, and Valerian moved on to perusing a nearby display of flowers.

"Before, you told me you thought Adeline had killed Steve because of those meetings in the alley," I said. "Now, I know you were there when they happened, so that's no longer a valid reason for suspecting her. What other evidence do you have, then?"

"I don't have any evidence." Gnorris looked down at the water that had spilled out of the watering can and idly traced the toe of his boot through it. "It's just a feeling. Plus..."

"Plus, what?"

"It's also a bit of sour grapes, maybe." Gnorris sighed again. "They cut me out. Steve told me he'd found a direct supplier for gelaroot, so he didn't need me to be the middleman anymore. Steve and Adeline knew cutting me out would mean bigger profits for each of them."

"That explains the sour grapes, but it's not a motive for Adeline to have murdered anyone." I didn't need to point out that it did, however, look like a motive for Gnorris to have killed Steve.

"Steve was getting more smug and selfish. He was so proud of what we were brewing, and he was telling more and more outside people about magic. It was dangerous, and Adeline was worried that if people began to believe Steve, they might figure out vampires were real, too."

"Why didn't you go to the constables with your suspicion?"

"I couldn't! Then I would have been forced to tell them how I knew this stuff. I was afraid to tell you, but I still wanted you to look into Adeline. I think she was scared, both of being discovered and of being the next one to be eliminated from the scheme, so she decided to act before things got out of control."

"What you three were doing isn't illegal, is it?" I asked. As I remembered it, there was nothing legally wrong with magical items passing into the mundane world. In fact, talking about magic and the supernatural weren't against the law, either. But, like Gnorris had said, most people would pass it off as tall tales.

"It's not illegal," Gnorris admitted. "But it's not considered good business practice, either. People here don't like anything that draws attention to the town, and if the love elixir became popular, it would mean more outside people talking about us. Plus, some people would view what we were doing as dishonest."

"Making magical potions for the non-magical world?" I asked.

"Yeah." Gnorris gestured toward the saplings. "I'm just trying to make a living. I thought it would be a good way to bring in some extra money. And, since it wasn't illegal, I convinced myself there was no harm in it."

"But you hadn't counted on Steve being so open about the plan." I had gone to the garden store thinking Gnorris wasn't the killer, but I was second-guessing myself. He seemed bitter about Steve's lack of discretion, and he was even more upset about being cut out of the deal.

What I needed, I realized, was to have another talk with Adeline. I would know exactly what kind of questions to ask the vampire this time around. But, considering our last meeting while I was on my backside in the alley, I wasn't keen on that. I didn't even want to go into the magic store after dark and risk seeing her.

It was clear Gnorris didn't have any more information he was willing to share, but he had already been more forthcoming than I had expected. I found Valerian about twenty feet away, browsing some small succulents in cute ceramic pots that looked like animals. As it turned out, she wasn't just pretending to shop, because she purchased a small aloe plant sprouting out of a kangaroo's pouch.

I filled Valerian in during the drive back to the funeral home, and she listened quietly. Every time I glanced at her, though, I could see the way her frown deepened.

"Gnorris is right," Valerian said when I finished. "There are a lot of us who would have been upset by this scheme. At least we have confirmation that Steve was telling the truth when he told James at the liquor distributor in Stanton about the drink."

"It's not just about drawing attention to Foxfire Haven and the fact magic exists, is it?" I asked.

"Magic of that kind is something that should only be worked on the willing," Valerian said without hesitation. "It's really unethical to work magic on someone if they're in the dark that magic even exists. Magical manipulation can get dangerous really fast."

"I remember we had to take a magical ethics class in middle school. I thought it was kind of a waste of time, because so much of it seemed obvious. Don't do revenge magic, only use herbs you're familiar with, and so forth."

"Magic is a big responsibility, but not everyone remembers that." Valerian fell silent, and I wondered if she was thinking of the potions she served—and sometimes made herself—at the tavern. There, of course, her patrons knew exactly what they were getting.

It was difficult to get anything done during the rest of the afternoon. Gnorris had given me information that felt like a physical burden. As the sun dropped toward the horizon, I knew what I had to do.

And it wasn't going to the magic store to talk to Adeline. It was something far worse.

Perkins was curled up in his nest in the kitchen, and I hated to rouse him from his sleep, but I needed his support. "Hey, little guy," I said as I nudged one of his wings with my index finger. "You want to go for a walk? That scary cat might come around, but I'll keep you safe."

Perkins cracked one yellow eye open, looking like he did not savor that idea one bit, but he dutifully stood and let me lift him to my shoulder.

I walked out the front door, down the circular driveway, and all the way to the sidewalk. As soon as I turned left, I felt a flow of soothing energy coming from Perkins. He had figured out where we were going, and he wanted to make me feel better about it.

Wyatt opened his door just a few seconds after I rang the bell. He leaned against the doorframe and looked from me to Perkins. "Yes?"

"I have information about Steve that might help your murder investigation." Wyatt didn't respond, so I told him about Steve, Gnorris, and Adeline going in together to make a magical elixir.

I didn't mention the part about it being aimed at the mundane world, and I wasn't sure why I held that tidbit back. Maybe it was because of my discussion with Valerian earlier. It was possible either Gnorris or Adeline was behind Steve's murder, but it was also possible they were both innocent. Their elixir venture had failed before it ever really got started, so there was no need to hurt their reputations if I didn't have to.

Wyatt remained silent for a long time after I finished. I was half-expecting him to slam the door in my face or tell me to stop wasting his time, so I was surprised when he said, "We didn't know the victim had any connection to Ms. Beaumont outside of him doing deliveries for her. This is good information."

"Great. I hope it helps you find the killer. Have a good evening." I turned to go, but Wyatt's commanding tone stopped me dead in my tracks.

"Stay out of it, Underwood. I appreciate the tip, but let the constables solve the case. You're taking this personally because the victim was found inside that rusty old—"

"Under."

"Under that hearse," Wyatt growled. "But let the professionals take care of this, okay?"

I wasn't about to go confront Adeline myself, and I couldn't think of who else I would want to talk to. That made it very easy to give Wyatt an honest answer. "I will."

When I made it to the sidewalk in front of Wyatt's house, I reached up to give Perkins a scratch. "Thanks, Perky. You really helped me stay calm. I'm going to take a walk before it gets completely dark, so why don't you head on home?"

Perkins hooted proudly, then fluttered into the air. As he headed toward home, I turned and walked in the opposite direction. I felt better now that I had shared the information about the elixir with Wyatt, but at the same time, I could feel the way my magic had been building up inside me all afternoon. It was a wonder I hadn't shed at all during my talk with Wyatt, and I chalked up that success to Perkins. He was so good at helping me stay in control.

The cool early evening air was invigorating. I felt refreshed as I continued to walk, and I could sense my body—and my magic—relaxing. With every step, I became more confident that I had my magic under control.

When I finally got home, the first stars were appearing in the sky. I stepped onto the front porch, looking forward to seeing my new friends and having a quiet evening, when I heard loud hooting.

I froze, one foot raised to go up the next step. The hooting continued, coming from the backyard, and it sounded like Perkins was in distress. My thoughts jumped to Wyatt's black cat, and I turned and ran down the steps and around the side of the house.

Perkins was there, standing on one side of the yard, the grass as high as his legs. He was still making short, loud sounds, but he was looking at the ground, and there wasn't a cat in sight.

I slowed my pace, since it was clear my familiar wasn't in immediate danger. My breath was coming in great rasps, even though I hadn't run very far.

Maybe I should start jogging instead of walking. Is fifty-three too old to take up jogging?

"What's the problem, Perky?" I crouched down next to the owl.

Perkins leaned down and pushed his face into a small hole. He was burrowing to create a new hangout for himself.

As I watched, Perkins disappeared inside the hole. I heard a dull clang, then he backed out and looked at me with a tilted head.

"Something is blocking the way," I guessed. "Probably a big rock. Let's dig it out."

I snaked my hand into the tunnel, and my fingers bumped against something solid. The object was smooth, and when I tapped a fingernail against it, I heard the same clang that had sounded when Perkins had tapped his beak against it before.

I began to dig, using my fingers since the object was only under about an inch of dirt. I cleared away the grass and soil, and soon, I could see that the object was a metal box, about six inches square.

Archer's confession that he and Roscoe had been looking for the same valuable item Uncle Grant had been so obsessed with popped into my memory. Had Perkins just found what so many people were after?

Twenty-Four

I HAD BEEN OUT of breath after running around the house, but I was downright breathless as I lifted the box out of its shallow hole. "Perkins, I think you might have found something really important," I said. "And, if I'm right, this might be why Steve was murdered."

In my mind, I saw Steve creeping around the property, searching everywhere for the alleged valuable item while someone watched from the shadows of the trees, waiting for the right moment to pounce.

I tried to open the hinged box, but the lid wouldn't budge. It had been in the ground too long to give way so easily. So, I went into the garage, where I expected there might be some tools I could use. Perkins followed along, eyeing the box that had hindered his burrowing.

It was strange going into the garage, since that was where Steve had been found. I had only taken a few steps into the garage the day I discovered Steve's body, and I had yet to explore the space further. I was still parking the hearse out front. There was a lamp on the workbench in front of the window, and I set the metal box next to it, then clicked on the lamp.

The box had rusted over the years, and no amount of tugging made the lid budge. Luckily, I found a toolkit on a nearby shelf, and soon, I had a hammer in my hand. I tapped against the lip of the lid with the hammer. The loud whine of metal grinding against metal told me I was on the right track.

It took another ten minutes of gentle hammering, but eventually, the lid popped open.

My Uncle Grant was staring back at me.

It was a photo of him as a very young man and several other people, all smiling happily. They were dressed nicely in clothes that had been in fashion about four decades before, and the colors in the photo had faded to sepia tones.

Underneath that was an envelope. I lifted it and the photo out of the box, still expecting to find the valuable item Grant had been so obsessed with during his final years. Instead, though, I found a small leather-bound photo book, a troll doll, a few magazine clippings about fads, and fourteen keychains, all from various tourist attractions around the country.

I pulled every single item out of the box before I realized that whatever I had found didn't have any value. I opened the envelope and pulled out a sheet of paper that was covered with neat, narrow handwriting.

The note explained that the Underwood family time capsule had been buried forty years before, and that it contained photos of family members as they had looked then, as well as information about things that were popular at the time.

In addition, Grant had written, *we have included a portion of our family keychain collection to commem-*

orate the places where we made some of our favorite memories.

I smiled down at the link to my family's past. The box did have something of value, after all. It just wasn't financial in nature. Carefully, I lowered the lid, ensuring I didn't seal it so tightly it would require tools to open it again.

"Thank you for finding this, Perky," I told my owl. He looked up at me and made a trilling noise that I had come to recognize as his way of conveying annoyance. In my mind, what he was telling me was *I did not find it, thank you very much. It was in my way.*

Perkins flew off the workbench and into the backyard, presumably so he could continue his burrowing.

Valerian was in the kitchen, standing in front of the sink as she slurped down a bowl of cereal. She swallowed, then waved her spoon in my direction. "Don't judge me! I just wanted a quick bite because I'm running late."

"No judgment here," I assured her. I rapped my knuckles against the metal box, which I had left on the countertop the night before. "Later, you can check out this old family time capsule Perkins found in the backyard."

"Oh, how fun! I'm working a double today, so it will be tomorrow before I can take a look." Valerian's smile quickly turned suspicious. "Do you think that's what Roscoe and Archer were after this whole time? Did they mistake Grant's interpretation of the word 'valuable'?"

"Possibly. But, if Grant was the one who buried the box, he would have known where to find it again. It doesn't make sense to me that he was searching for it like his life depended on it." I absently rubbed my thumb over a rusty spot on the box. "No, I believe the valuable item is still hidden."

"If it wasn't simply some delusion of your uncle's." Valerian's voice was soft, and she stepped close so she could put a hand on my arm. "If his behavior was as odd as people are saying it was, the thing he was searching for might have never existed in the first place."

"I know. However, that's not going to stop people like Roscoe and Archer from looking for it. So, if you see anyone digging holes in my backyard, and it's not Perkins, call the constables."

Valerian laughed as she dropped her arm and returned to her cereal.

After Valerian left for the tavern, I prepared to settle in for a quiet day of getting things done around the house and doing a bit of weeding in the front flowerbed. The only interruption I had was from Petunia, who called in the afternoon to ask if I'd deliver some plants to a client at eight o'clock that evening. She explained the customer was a vampire, so I couldn't make the delivery until after dark.

Prior to that, though, my evening was promising to be as quiet as my day had been. Marlee had texted to say she would be late because she was having dinner with a friend, and although I didn't know where Jo was, she had yet to come home.

Once the sun had set, I decided to get in some serious relaxation time before I had to leave for the garden store delivery. I grabbed a book and a fuzzy blanket, and I had just read the first sentence of the book when my phone rang.

It was Valerian. "Hey. I just had a quick dinner break, and I have to tell you what I saw on the drive back to the tavern." Valerian's voice was muffled, and I wondered if she was trying to avoid being overheard. "I just saw Adeline and Gnorris at the park in front of the town hall. They looked really suspicious, glancing around like they were up to something. Plus, Gnorris was covered in dirt and grass stains! Even from the street I could tell how dirty he was. I don't know what they're up to, but you might want to come into town."

That news made zero sense to me. Gnorris was angry about being cut out of the magic potion scheme, and he was convinced Adeline had killed Steve. Why in the world would he meet up with her?

"Thanks. I'm not sure I want to walk into the middle of whatever they're doing, but I'll ask Gnorris about it tomorrow," I said. "I'll talk to you later."

I was beginning to pull the phone away from my ear when Valerian hissed, "Wait!"

"What?"

"Gnorris just walked in! Come to the tavern, and pretend you're just hanging out. It's a perfect chance to talk to him."

I looked wistfully at my book. It didn't seem to matter whether I talked to Gnorris right that moment or the next day. Plus, I had promised Wyatt I wouldn't go looking for answers about Steve's murder.

But, I hadn't promised not to go to the tavern and have a drink.

My curiosity was winning out over my common sense. "I'll be there in fifteen minutes," I told Valerian.

When I walked into the tavern, the first thing I did was scan the long bar in search of Gnorris. He was seated near the far end, just a few stools away from where Barry the Bigfoot usually perched. While Barry had always looked awkwardly large for the barstool, Gnorris was much too small. He sat on the very edge of the stool, with just his nose and eyes rising above the edge of the bar. He had a small glass in his hands filled with what looked like beer.

I began walking toward the empty stool next to Gnorris, but just before I reached it, there was a tap on my shoulder. I turned to see Archer standing there. He had taken off the baseball cap he'd been wearing, and he was turning it around in his hands.

"Hazel, um." Archer stopped and turned his head to stare at the dart board.

I waited patiently while Archer took a couple of deep breaths. He swallowed hard, then said, "I think it's my fault Steve Zillmann wound up dead in your garage."

TWENTY-FIVE

I FORGOT ALL ABOUT Gnorris and Adeline as I stared at Archer, my mouth open. Was he confessing to killing Steve, right here in the middle of the tavern?

"You see," Archer said, still not looking at me, "when you hired me, I realized it was the perfect opportunity to look around inside the funeral home. Since, you know, Roscoe and I searched the grounds but didn't break in to look around the home itself."

"I remember you telling me that," I said, surprised Archer wanted to clear his name of breaking and entering, even though he might be on the verge of confessing to murder.

"I grabbed that ring of keys hanging near the back door when you weren't looking. I found the one that opened the garage doors, but there was no body when I was in there."

I nodded. "That explains how you knew about the old sockets in there. I thought it was strange you mentioned them, since the garage had been locked since I arrived in town."

"And that's the problem. Later, I realized I had forgotten to lock up when I was done. But I wasn't scheduled to do any work at your place, so I figured I'd just do it the next time I was there and you weren't looking. But, before I could lock up, you found Steve."

"I'm not happy to know you were sneaking into locked areas of my property, but this doesn't explain why it's your fault Steve died." Archer's news did, at least, explain why the garage doors had been unlocked when I had gone out there to inspect the hearse.

"I'm not saying it's my fault he was killed," Archer said quickly. "But, I do think it's my fault he wound up in your garage. Someone killed him, then hid his body in there. If I had locked up properly, you wouldn't be dealing with all this."

"If the garage had been locked, the killer would have found some other hiding place nearby. Behind the bushes, or maybe back in the wooded area behind the funeral home. Don't feel bad that the garage wound up being the spot the killer chose."

Archer looked relieved, and he gave me a faint smile. "You're not mad?"

"I'm not mad. But, at the same time, I might work with a different electrician from here on out. Someone who won't sneak into my locked garage, looking for treasure."

Archer had been so eager to tell me he and Roscoe had never engaged in breaking and entering. As it turned out, Archer had skipped the breaking part and gone right for entering. If I couldn't trust him to stay out of my garage, who knew where else he might try to go? No, I couldn't risk him possibly rummaging through my belongings, or those of my roommates.

It was too bad. Archer did good work, and his rates were reasonable.

A memory from more than a week before popped into my head. "You snuck into the funeral home one morning last week, didn't you? Jo found my front door wide open, but it should have been closed and locked."

Archer looked at me curiously. "No, that wasn't me. I don't have a key to your front door."

"Then how did it—"

"Stop talking to her!"

I whirled around to see Roscoe sitting at the last booth in the tavern, his torso leaning out as he raised a finger toward Archer. "She might put a curse on you if you cross her path. Don't you know what she did out behind the magic store?"

"That was an accident!" I snapped. "What makes you think I would curse anyone?"

Roscoe laughed sharply. "I figure you're as cracked as Grant was. Probably runs in the family."

"Settle down, Roscoe!" The voice was Jo's.

"Yeah. You can't talk to our friend that way!" Marlee said as she and Jo appeared on either side of me.

At the same time, Valerian came out from behind the bar to join us. "Do you want to be permanently banned from the tavern, Roscoe?"

Roscoe sneered and began to slide farther into the booth, but he stopped and glared at the four of us. A new fire was in his eyes as he stood up and took several steps forward. Archer hastily jumped backward, so he wasn't trapped between Roscoe and four witches.

Marlee and Jo each grabbed one of my hands. I pulled my gaze away from Roscoe long enough to see Marlee's other hand in Valerian's.

"Sure, take her side," Roscoe drawled. "You'll see. When she starts to get—"

Roscoe never got to finish his sentence because a pulse of bright-pink magic shot out of me, right in his direction.

Except, this time, I wasn't embarrassed, and I didn't feel out of control. To my left, a wave of purple magic emanated from Jo. Marlee's sparkling dark-red magic looked beautiful next to Valerian's golden wave.

Our combined magic rushed forward, then stopped just inches from Roscoe. Slowly, the magic drifted downward, piling onto the floor briefly before dissipating. We hadn't hurt Roscoe, but we had given him a stern warning.

Roscoe's eyes widened, and he wisely kept his mouth shut. He took another step forward, then turned on his heel as he mumbled, "I'll go out the back."

As Roscoe disappeared out the back door, all four of us started to laugh. The entire tavern had fallen silent during the confrontation, and suddenly, everyone seemed to start talking at once. A few people even clapped.

Jo squeezed my hand. "Look who's feeling confident now."

I was grinning so hard my face hurt. "That was amazing."

Two people moved to different barstools so Jo, Marlee, and I could sit in a row at the bar. I wound up exactly where I had hoped to be when I had come in the door: Gnorris was to my right.

Valerian got back to work serving drinks while Marlee and I talked about what a feat we had just pulled off. Jo wasn't listening. Instead, she was leaning so far back I worried she would topple off the stool. Her head craned around, like she was looking for someone.

"That was impressive," Gnorris said to me once Marlee and I had quieted down. "Can I buy you a beer for giving that old grump exactly what he deserved?"

"I've got to make a delivery in a bit," I said. "But you can buy me a diet soda."

"You're a cheap date." Gnorris started to laugh, then gave me a frightened look. "That was just a joke. You and your friends don't need to come after me, too."

"You're not in any trouble with us," I assured him.

"I heard about that incident behind Into the Cauldron. It sounds like you shed a lot of magic."

"Everyone in this town knows, don't they?" I leaned forward and put my elbows on the bar, then rested my forehead in my hands.

"Cheer up," Gnorris said. "What you ladies just did is going to be the hot gossip now, so everyone will forget about your little accident."

In answer, I just sighed.

"I'm the only gnome in Foxfire Haven," Gnorris continued. "I know how it feels to be on the outside. How you've been feeling since you got here. But you're lucky, because now you've got those three on your side. The four of you are going to be a powerful coven."

That got me to lift my head. "I think you're right," I said. "I'm grateful to have them. By the way, you're a bit of a mess."

Gnorris picked at a streak of dirt on the sleeve of his white sweater. "Eh, I was doing some foraging earlier."

"Foraging for gelaroot?"

"Maybe." Gnorris gave me a sly look. "If I can source it myself instead of going to my supplier, then I can save a lot of money."

"You and Adeline are teaming up again, even though you think she killed Steve?"

"No way! I'm trying to create my own elixir."

"Then why were you and Adeline meeting in the park just before you came here?"

Gnorris chuckled. "Of course you already know about that. See what I mean about the town gossip moving on from your incident? Adeline called me late last night, upset because Chief Constable Hightower called her and asked some difficult questions. She accused me of pointing the authorities in her direction."

I tried very hard to keep my expression neutral, but one corner of my lip began to twitch.

Gnorris gave a slight nod, like I had just confirmed his suspicion. "I told her I hadn't discussed anything with the constables, but that I'd be open to talking it out, anyway. I insisted on meeting out in public, because there was no way I was going to risk being her next victim."

"You said that to her?"

"No. I'm not stupid. Anyway, I reassured her that I hadn't said anything to the constables, and I implied they must have heard reports of Steve blabbing about our business venture to outside people."

I reached out and plucked a leaf off of Gnorris's red hat. "You said you were foraging. Were you doing it in my backyard?"

Gnorris's eyes lit up. "You have gelaroot?"

I waved the leaf. "Actually, I...Oh." I turned slightly and grabbed Marlee's hand excitedly. She automatically lifted her other hand and placed it in Jo's.

Valerian hustled toward us and reached over the bar to complete the circle. "I have no idea what's happening," she said, "but I feel like I should be a part of it."

"I'm not sure, either," I admitted. "But, right now, I need your support and encouragement."

"For what?" Marlee asked. She looked over her shoulder, like there might be someone threatening approaching.

"I have to make a delivery tonight, and then I'm going straight to the police. I think I know who killed Steve."

Twenty-Six

"Don't wait!" Valerian said. "Go to the police, right now!"

I shook my head slowly. "No. I want to think this over before I say anything. It's a wild theory, and I don't want to accuse someone of murder unless I am absolutely sure they're guilty." I glanced at my watch. "I need to get going."

"Who needs a delivery run at night?"

"A vampire, of course."

Valerian shrugged. "The customer could have been a troll. They don't like daylight."

I wasn't sure if Valerian was joking or not. I had thought trolls were just legends, and I certainly couldn't picture a troll who liked to garden.

Quickly, I thanked Gnorris for the soda. He seemed stunned by what I'd said to my roommates, and the only response I got from him were blurts of surprise.

Jo and Marlee were sliding off their barstools.

"I'll drive separately," Marlee said. "Jo and I will follow you to make sure you get safely to the constables."

"I wish I could go," Valerian lamented. "In fact...Hey, Will! Can you cover for me? It's kind of urgent."

The tavern's owner was at the other end of the bar, and he hollered for Valerian to go for it.

"I'll take my own car," Valerian told me, "in case things run long and I need to get back to work."

A few minutes later, I was driving down Main Street with both Marlee and Valerian driving their cars behind me. When I rolled up to a stop sign, I spotted Wyatt standing on the corner, chatting with someone. I rolled down my window and yelled his name.

"Follow us!" I told Wyatt. "I'm picking up plants for a delivery, and then we're going to have a chat about Steve's murder." I had said I would mull over my theory before going to the constables, but seeing Wyatt was a reminder that I was supposed to be letting the professionals solve the case. Plus, I was feeling too anxious to wait until after the delivery was complete.

Wyatt's car was parked on the curb, and soon, we had what felt like a funeral procession rolling down Main Street, with my hearse followed by three cars.

I pulled up right in front of the garden store, and the other cars stayed in line behind me. When I got out of the hearse, Petunia came out the front door and gestured to the vehicles. "Do you need this much help for six plants?"

I had told myself I wasn't going to say anything. I really had intended to go through with picking up the plants, then turning everything over to the constables. But, with my roommates and Wyatt walking up next to me, I felt emboldened.

I was also feeling more certain my hunch was correct.

"They're my moral support," I said. "Tell me, what happened to your Autumn Frost bushes?"

Petunia gave me a surprised look. "What?"

"You mentioned they had disappeared, so you couldn't fulfill the order for the Watkins estate. They were stolen, weren't they? Because Autumn Frost and gelaroot are the same thing, and Steve needed it to make his magic elixir."

"Magic elixir?" Petunia glanced at my roommates, as if to confirm she'd heard me correctly. "Steve was our delivery guy. He wasn't a potions expert."

"No, but he had Adeline for that. Autumn Frost is too big to steal with a regular car. It had to be taken in a van or a truck. You suspected Steve of swiping your entire inventory of Autumn Frost during one of his deliveries for you, so you followed him, right to another source of the plant: the funeral home."

Petunia paled. "No."

"The only thing I don't understand," I pressed, "is why you killed Steve. They were just plants."

Wyatt stepped toward Petunia, then glanced at me. "You're making some big assumptions, Underwood."

"I know," I said quietly.

Petunia looked at Wyatt, and I saw a tear slide down her cheek. "Please."

"I'm not going to arrest you based on some vague theory," Wyatt assured her. Still, I could hear the doubt in his voice.

"It was an accident, wasn't it?" I asked. "You didn't mean to kill Steve."

Petunia buried her face in her hands, and she began to sob. After a few moments, she lifted her head, her eyes bloodshot from crying. "The back of his truck was open when I pulled up behind it at the funeral home, and all my Autumn Frost bushes were inside. I found Steve in the backyard, taking cuttings of the plants. I confronted him, and we argued. He lunged at me with gardening shears, so I grabbed a vine of ivy that was growing up the garage wall and looped it around his neck the next time he came at me."

I heard a squeak from one of my roommates. Marlee had both hands pressed over her mouth, staring in horror at Petunia.

"The vine shouldn't have killed him," Petunia continued. "I just wanted to scare him. But I'm a garden witch, and my magic was building up with my fear and stress, and the vine started to tighten. I was strangling him with my magic, and I couldn't stop it."

My heart lurched in my chest. Petunia had experienced her own magical exhalation, but hers had been deadly. I had been very lucky that the worst damage mine had done was to my ego.

Wyatt pressed his lips together, and I was surprised that he looked more sad than angry. "You dragged his body into the garage, then stashed his truck down a dirt lane five miles outside of town. We found it this morning, but there were no plants inside it."

"Of course not," Petunia said. "I knew if anyone found the plants inside Steve's truck, they would suspect me. So, I hauled them into the forest and left them." She fixed me with a bitter stare. "No one should have suspected me. I don't understand how you put it all together."

"Those answers can wait until later," Wyatt said. Petunia didn't protest as he stepped behind her and put her in handcuffs.

It wasn't until Wyatt was driving away with Petunia sitting dejectedly in the back of the constable car that any of us spoke. It was Jo who broke the silence. "How *did* you put the pieces together? I never would have thought Petunia was capable of murder!"

"Me, neither," I admitted. "If I had, I would have told her to find someone else to deliver her plants! When I picked up my first delivery for the store, Petunia said several Autumn Frost bushes were supposed to be included, but she couldn't find them. I realized from her description that I had the same plant growing by my garage."

"And you solved the murder based on *that*?" Marlee asked in an awed tone.

"No. It was Gnorris who helped me put it together. He had referenced the plant used for the magic potion as gelaroot. Tonight, at the bar, I picked a leaf off his hat, and that was the name he used for it. However, I recognized the leaf as what I have in my backyard, and I realized the same plant has two different names. Steve was involved in a business scheme that needed gelaroot, and his body was found right next to some. It couldn't be a coincidence. My guess is that Steve was roaming around the funeral home property at some point, looking for that same alleged treasure that Roscoe and Archer are after. Steve spotted the plant and started harvesting it."

"He cut out Gnorris as the middleman and resorted to stealing the Autumn Frost from the funeral home," Jo said. She was writing in her reporter's notebook, no doubt recording every detail for her forthcoming bombshell of a newspaper article. "After you moved into the funeral home, Steve probably realized he needed to find a new source for the plant. Even after he stole Petunia's plants, he was so greedy that instead of cutting Gnorris back into the deal, he made one last harvest run at the funeral home, probably doing it when you were out running errands."

"And since you hadn't killed Steve yourself, that left Petunia as the last suspect standing," Valerian said.

"I still thought it was entirely possible Adeline or Gnorris had done it," I said. "But once I made the connection between the plant and the potion, I had a gut feeling I was right. My plan was to mull it all over while I made this delivery for Petunia, and I figured I could ask her a few questions to help me decide if my theory was strong enough to present to the constables."

"But with Wyatt standing right there, you went for it, and she crumbled." Jo was grinning. "We are so going to celebrate tonight!"

"We're also going to do a gratitude ritual," Valerian said, "because we're grateful this is all over. First, though, I need to get back to work."

I gestured toward the store. "And I have a plant delivery to make first."

"Jo and I will help you," Marlee said. "And we'll lock up the store behind us. Once Valerian gets home from the tavern tonight, we'll do the ritual."

"Good plan," I said. "And, I think I've solved our problem about calling the corners. Everyone wanted air, since our familiars are birds. But Perkins is a burrowing owl. He lives in the earth. Stella is a tropical bird, so she's built for hot climates."

"Like fire!" Marlee said happily.

"And Gordon is a pelican, meaning he's related to water," Jo said, her eyes lighting up.

Valerian laughed. "Which leaves me and Lonnie to represent air. Look at us! A coven of crones!"

"With our feathered familiars!" Jo said.

Marlee lifted her arms and mimicked flying. "Birds of a feather!"

I grinned. "Crones of a feather!"

Twenty-Seven

I SHUT THE REAR of the hearse with a satisfied *bang*. Will was wheeling the last of the beer crates into the tavern on a cart, and I was done with a solid day's work. I'd had four deliveries to make during that day, beginning at eight o'clock in the morning.

Business was good.

And, in the month since Steve's murder had been solved, the buzz about him had finally died down. At first, my clients would bring up his name every time I arrived to pick something up. "Oh, poor Steve" and "Steve used to..." had been uttered so often I had started hearing the words in my sleep.

As one week had led into the next, though, my clients had shifted to talking about the increased rain as we got deeper into the fall and how nice the town hall looked with the fresh white paint on the cupola.

I stretched, then covered a yawn. "It's only six o'clock, Haze," I lectured myself. Marlee had texted the rest of the coven to say she needed some relaxing time with us, so we had agreed to meet her at the tavern. I bounced on the balls of my feet to wake myself up a bit, then headed inside.

Marlee was already sitting at the bar, halfway through a glass of wine.

"Hey," I said, hopping up onto the stool next to her. "You said something about your high-maintenance client in your text. Everything okay?"

Marlee pressed a hand to her stomach. "I had a cake-tasting session with her this afternoon. I'm not going to need food for three days."

Valerian swept up to us just then, already pouring a glass of chardonnay for me. "Oh, the torture," she intoned.

"Normally I wouldn't complain, since Karla makes such great cakes, but this was my client's third tasting! The wedding is still a month away, and it can't come soon enough." Marlee wiggled her shoulders, like she was shaking off the negative energy.

So, naturally, Valerian and I leaned as far away from her as we could.

"Don't worry," Marlee assured us. "I shed all that excess empathy magic outside. You're not going to get any on you."

Valerian and I relaxed as I said, "If she decides on a fourth tasting, Val and I would be happy to help."

"I'd love to give my input on cake," Valerian agreed.

"What about cake?" Jo appeared to Marlee's right. I wasn't sure she heard the answer, because she was looking around the tavern expectantly. Then, with a small shrug, she sat down. "I'm glad it was a slow news day! Otherwise, I wouldn't have made it here so early."

Valerian made a few drinks for other customers, then came back to our spot at the bar. "Now that you're all here, I wanted to ask how you all feel about a house-cleaning spell. I thought we could create one to cut down on the amount of dirt, dust, and soap scum we have to tackle."

Jo leaned forward so she could get a good look at me. "Hazel?"

I nodded. "I'm willing to give it a try. What's the worst that will happen?" I gave a weak laugh. "It can't be more disastrous than that home security spell we tried last week."

Working magic again was proving to be harder than I'd expected. Not only was I battling my uncontrolled magical exhalations, but I was also struggling to re-learn everything. Magic was so much more than say-ing an incantation or making a potion. It was also about intention, focus, and control.

My intentions were good. It was the focus and con-trol parts I was struggling with. Luckily, my room-mates were being very patient with me.

No, not my roommates. My coven.

Marlee and Jo began discussing whether it was bet-ter to use mint or sage to minimize shower scum. As they were talking, I spun slowly on my stool, taking in the cozy tavern and the people sitting and talking with each other. It had taken a while, but I was be-ginning to feel like I belonged in Foxfire Haven again.

Roscoe and Archer were at their usual booth, huddled together and talking about who knew what. I didn't let it bother me. I had told Archer about the discovery of the family time capsule in the backyard, but, like me, he didn't seem to think that had been the valuable item my Uncle Grant had been so desperately looking for.

Nevertheless, Archer had promised he wouldn't look for the item anymore.

It wasn't like he would have had much of an opportunity, anyway. I had hired the only other electrician in town, after ensuring he wasn't an amateur treasure hunter, too.

Uncle Grant's obsession and erratic behavior remained a mystery, but I wasn't going to be inviting anyone to dig holes in my backyard anytime soon.

The front door of the tavern opened, and Barry stepped inside. I glanced down the bar to see that his usual spot was free, and I wondered if the locals typically avoided sitting there on purpose. I'd only seen it occupied by someone other than Barry once, and that had been when every other stool was taken.

When I looked at the front door again, Barry had turned around, the door slowly closing behind him as he left.

"Huh," Valerian said. I spun to face her, and she gave a little shrug. "He's never done that before."

She walked away, and I returned my attention to Jo and Marlee. They were still deep in discussion about herbs, but they had moved on to which one would be best for keeping mirrors streak-free.

Valerian had to work the late shift, but the rest of us headed home to make dinner a short while later. Marlee was in better spirits, and I was so tired I considered skipping dinner altogether so I could fall into bed.

The funeral home was so full of life as I chopped vegetables, Marlee got a pot of water boiling, and Jo doled out beverages. Our familiars even came inside to help, flying through a kitchen window we kept cracked open so they could come and go.

Lonnie cawed loudly, which I interpreted as her asking where her witch was.

"Valerian won't be home until late," I told the raven. After I gave Perkins a kiss on the top of his head, I reached out and stroked Lonnie's glossy black feathers. "But we're happy to have you with us."

Lonnie clicked her beak and stepped closer to Perkins. Gordon and Stella followed suit, until the four of them were shoulder-to-shoulder in a line.

It was adorable.

When dinner was ready and we sat down at the dining room table to eat, the familiars followed us and fluttered into place on their perch. We had made the perch out of a fallen branch and old sawhorses I had found in the garage, and the hulking thing sat in one corner of the room.

As I got ready for bed that night, I reflected on how much my life had changed in the short time I had been back in Foxfire Haven. It had been nearly two months since I had arrived at the derelict funeral home, feeling dejected. Now, I had so much to be grateful for.

I smiled at myself in the bathroom mirror as I brushed my hair. "I guess we need to do another gratitude ritual," I murmured.

"Just don't use that incense again, please."

I turned around to see Holman pulling a face of absolute disgust. "Ghosts can smell?" I asked.

"Of course we can. Speaking of which, I've been meaning to tell Jo to lay off that perfume of hers. It makes her smell like a pine tree."

Holman disappeared, and I shook my head, knowing Jo was about to get a visit from him.

Yes, my life was very different. And very good. My only real complaint was that the front door had been found wide open two more times in the past month, with no reasonable explanation.

I finished up in the bathroom and was snapping off the hallway light when the doorbell rang. I glanced at the antique wooden clock on the wall. It was nearly eleven o'clock. Who could possibly be paying us a visit so late? I instantly worried something bad had happened, and someone had come to tell me about it.

As I made my way toward the front door, I told myself it probably wasn't an emergency. Maybe Valerian had forgotten her keys. Or, perhaps, Wyatt had decided to apologize to me for being such a cranky neighbor.

No, that was a ridiculous notion. He'd been happily ignoring me ever since Steve's murder had been solved.

I braced myself for whatever was about to happen, then opened the front door.

Nothing could have prepared me for what greeted me. Tara stood there, looking scared. Her long brown hair was messy, like she hadn't bothered to brush it in a while. Her gray eyes, which looked so much like my own, were wide.

"Gamma!" Hailey was standing at the bottom of the steps, her hand in her father's. Brian looked frightened, too, but Hailey was bouncing with delight.

My mouth went dry as I looked at Tara again. "What's wrong?"

Tara glanced at Hailey, then stepped closer to me. "Hailey nearly blew up her preschool this morning. She needs your help, Mom."

A NOTE FROM THE AUTHOR

Thank you for traveling all the way to the Pacific Northwest for your first visit to Foxfire Haven! I hope you enjoyed meeting Hazel and the other witches as much as I did.

This series is proof that inspiration can come from anywhere. My husband and I spent the night in a former funeral home during a stopover in Chicago, and after waking up in the former embalming room, I knew exactly where Hazel was going to live when she returned to her hometown. Of course, Jo got the room with the sloping floor, like the one Ed and I slept in!

If you're feeling a bit inspired, too, please consider leaving a review. Indie authors like me rely on reviews to help readers find our books.

Eternally Yours,

P.S. You can keep up with my latest book news, get fun freebies, and more by signing up for my newsletter at BethDolgner.com!

Next in Series

Find out what's next for Hazel and the Crones of a Feather!

Divination and Deceit
Crones of a Feather Paranormal Cozy Mysteries Book 2

Frozen peas, political rivalries, and a body in the park. Magic and murder collide in Foxfire Haven.

There's a sudden vacancy on the Foxfire Haven City Council when Fortie Fortenbacher is found dead in the park. Euphoria Lachlan, the mayor of Foxfire Haven and Hazel Underwood's high-school bully, is wasting no time finding a replacement. Did Euphoria permanently remove Fortie from the council?

Hazel claims she's not trying to solve the murder, but she keeps stumbling onto clues as she drives her vintage hearse from one delivery job to the next. A Bigfoot with surprising insight, a witch who sees the future in frozen peas, and a shifter eager to pick up where Fortie left off will all help point Hazel toward the killer.

While Hazel tries to navigate the political infighting in a magical small town, she and her coven are also eager to find out if the fates foreseen for them will come true. And will Hazel and Chief Constable Hightower ever learn to get along?

Acknowledgments

As always, I am grateful to the amazing team that helped get this book out into the world. My test readers—Kristine, Sabrina, Alex, David, Lisa, and Mom—gave me early feedback to make the story better. My street team and ARC readers help get things rolling leading up to and on launch day.

Lia at Your Best Book Editor and Trish at Blossoming Pages made sure everything looked polished with their superb editing skills.

And a special thanks goes to Martin Atkins and the Museum of Post Punk and Industrial Music. Without the chance to spend the night in the funeral-home-turned-museum, there would be no Taylor Brothers Funeral Home, no Uncle Grant, and—more importantly—no Holman to show up and be snarky.

BOOKS BY BETH DOLGNER

Crones of a Feather
Paranormal Cozy Mystery Series
Spells and Subterfuge
Divination and Deceit
Manifesting and Mischief

Nightmare, Arizona
Paranormal Cozy Mystery Series
Homicide at the Haunted House
Drowning at the Diner
Slaying at the Saloon
Murder at the Motel
Poisoning at the Party
Headless at Halloween (Novella)
Clawing at the Corral
Axing at the Antique Store
Fatality at the Festival
Terminated at the Trailhead
Body at the Bakery

Eternal Rest Bed and Breakfast
Paranormal Cozy Mystery Series

Sweet Dreams
Late Checkout
Picture Perfect
Destination Wedding (Novella)
Scenic Views
Breakfast Included
Groups Welcome
Quiet Nights
Halloween Vibes (Novella)

Betty Boo, Ghost Hunter
Romantic Urban Fantasy Series
Ghost of a Threat
Ghost of a Whisper
Ghost of a Memory
Ghost of a Hope

Manifest
Young Adult Steampunk

A Talent for Death
Young Adult Urban Fantasy

Non-fiction
Georgia Spirits and Specters
Everyday Voodoo

ABOUT THE AUTHOR

BETH DOLGNER'S CAREER AS an author began in nonfiction with *Georgia Spirits and Specters*, a collection of Georgia ghost stories. From there, Beth entered the world of ghost hunting and was a longtime guide with the Roswell Ghost Tour in Georgia. She also lectures on Victorian death and mourning customs as well as Victorian Spiritualism, which stemmed from her volunteer work with Atlanta's Historic Oakland Cemetery. Beth likes to think of it all as research for her books.

Outside of writing, Beth enjoys traveling, sewing, and trying to convince her husband, Ed, that ghosts are real.

Keep up with Beth and sign up for her newsletter at BethDolgner.com.